INNER-CITY
GIRL

Colleen Smith-Dennis

Editors: Nicola Brown & K. Sean Harris
Cover Illustration: Courtney Lloyd Robinson
Cover Design: Sanya Dockery
Book Design, Layout & Typesetting: Sanya Dockery

Published by LMH Publishing Limited
Suite 10-11
LOJ Industrial Complex
7 Norman Road
Kingston C.S.O., Jamaica
Tel.: (876) 938-0005; 938-0712
Fax: (876) 759-8752
Email: lmhbookpublishing@cwjamaica.com
Website: www.lmhpublishing.com

Printed in the U.S.A.   ISBN: 978-976-8202-65-9

One

"But Miss Turner, mi nuh understand why Martina go behind mi back an' choose school inna big claas people area when so much school down ya so!" exclaimed Miss Fuller.

Miss Turner listened intently. Her fair skin was beginning to show her age, many dark blotches had sprung up all over her body and her face bore innumerable minute lines which crisscrossed all over her face. She always crinkled her face as if everything was a big puzzle to her and whenever she spoke it was as if the words pricked her tongue and caused her great pain so she spoke in a slow measured manner. Her eyes seemed to be disappearing into her face and even when she opened them wide, they still seemed to be a far distance away.

"But Miss Fuller di gal do well! She pass fi go a big school!" spoke Miss Turner, in what for her was an excited tone.

Miss Fuller turned to look at her and one could see a look which was distantly akin to a smile slowly appearing at the corner of her eyes. Unlike Miss Turner's eyes, hers were huge, too huge and bold. She could hold a person's stare for minutes without blinking. Those who knew her thought that "puss bruk coconut in her eye". She was too bold and brazen about everything; her eyes, her makeup, her gold wig and her mode of dressing loudly bellowed her character.

At the moment she was dressed in a blue shorts which hugged her bottom like a second skin and greatly emphasized her body contours. The lower parts of the cheeks of her bottom had escaped the brief shorts and were staring boldly like her huge eyes. The blouse she wore adequately covered her breasts and no more. Her navel, like a finger in the middle of her belly, bravely pointed its way forward; it was surrounded by long white lines deeply fixed in her belly. She spoke too loudly, always as if everyone had a hearing impairment or somehow lacked understanding and had to be shouted at. She looked boldly at Miss Turner now, the smile still present at the corner of her eyes.

"Yes mi proud of har but weh mi ago get all of dat money fi sen' har go up deh so. Mi no have dem kine a money deh!"

As she spoke, her voice became louder and louder and some of the neighbours who were in their yards and those passing by turned to look at them. This did not daunt her in any way. She continued, "Is only me one. Mi nuh have nobody fi help mi an' the other two haffi go a school to. Mi caa spen' out all a wha mi no have pon her."

She drew nearer to Miss Turner as she spoke, as if daring her to provide a solution to her problems. Miss Turner crinkled her face even more as she strove to find an answer. The words came out even slower than before as she spoke. "Fully, she have to go to school. You caa mek she stay here an' waste har ability. She have to go a school. You have to find a way!"

She was standing up now, arms akimbo and looking straight into Miss Fuller's eyes. Miss Fuller stared back, her eyes becoming even bigger than before. "Well Miss T, me done decide say she ago go right down the road an' not a inch farther! Big pass or no big pass she a go right down the road!"

"Gal, but lissen to me." Miss Turner's words came out almost like an ordinary speaker. This only happened when she was angry and she was angry now. "Miss Fuller, I don't say anyt'ing wrong wid Rockwell Comprehensive but the little gal pass fi go somewhere better, sen' her gwaan! Give her a chance in life and don't put nuh block in her way. She work hard an' she have good head piece, nuh stifle her! Sit down little bit an' let wi talk."

She sat on the top step close to her front door and pointed to the step below it, indicating that Miss Fuller should sit there. She did and the discussion continued. "Miss Fuller, try wid you daughter. Try wid her. You know that most a de young gal dem who go down a dat school no come out at all! Before dem reach fourteen is belly dem get. The—"

"But Miss Turner, whether she go up the big school or down a Rockwell a same place here so she a go live; so whatever she mus' get she will get!" Miss Fuller interjected heatedly.

Miss Turner stood up and pointed straight in Miss Fuller's face. "What you trying to do, mash up de gal life like how you mash up yours? She never ask you to mash up your life so gi her a chance. Try with her an' seek help and God will provide the rest." Miss Turner sat down after making this speech. She was breathing hard and her face was more crinkled than ever.

It was now Miss Fuller's time to stand and clinch her point. "You t'ink sey me want every nayga inna dis here place to tell me say a dem mine my pickney. You want them to torment out her life and drop word fi har every time dem see har?" As she spoke her eyes widened like ripples spreading in a pond. She bent her body forward to emphasize each word, revealing even more of the cheeks of her bottom much to the pleasure of the passers-by.

"I not talking 'bout these people roun' here. You well know dat everybody roun' here that have pickney a go a high school ask Daddy Pinnado fi help dem and him always help dem. Even the school fee him will help you with," said Miss Turner in a matter of fact voice. Patrick Pinnado, called Daddy Pinnado by the residents of the community, was the Member of Parliament for the area.

"But is not school fee alone she need fi go up there. She need other t'ings like uniform, book an' shoes."

"You know what wrong wid you? You give up before you even start. We know dat life hard especially down here but dat no sey you mus' give up without fighting. You are a woman or what! Woman and mother born to fight life! Memba dis, woman born to struggle!" With that she got up and went inside her house.

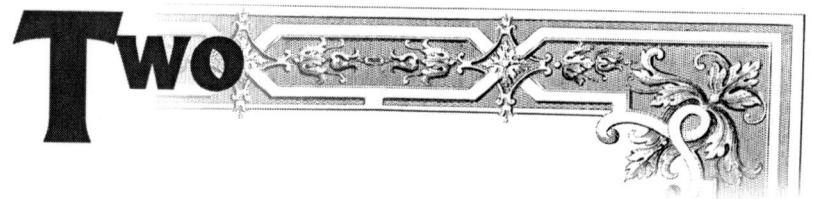

Two

Martina sat in the corner of the small room she shared with her fourteen year old brother Shimron and ten year old sister Yvette. She had heard bits and pieces of the conversation between Miss Turner and her mother. It came to her like a boat dipping in and out, down and up on a rough sea, her mother's voice always the one riding the waves. At first she was sitting on the bed but when she heard her mother's voice she went and sat in the corner.

For this slight, milo complexioned eleven year old girl with the oval face and saturnine looks, the corner beside the single bed she shared with her sister had become a kind of meditative asylum. Whenever there was anything to give serious thought to or if her spirit had been trampled, she would sit in her corner and think or read. Her mother considered this habit quite morbid and often told her that for a little girl she was too gloomy. She ascribed this gloominess to the fact that she read too many books and spoke too little. Yet it was this same mother who threatened to murder her if she got mixed up or allowed any man to play with her. "Life hard enough already, an' I don't want any more crosses on top a my crosses. Any time you forget say you a little gal you have to fine you way out!"

Tina understood some of what she was saying but not all. One thing that was as plain as poverty was that boys were as dangerous as the frequent gunshots that could be heard at nights. From her corner, she surveyed the room; it was about nine feet by nine feet and its furnishings comprised of two single beds, one which she shared with her sister and the other which belonged to her brother. The only other piece of furniture uncomfortably squeezed into a corner was a three-draw chest of drawers which appeared to have more bruises and cuts than Miss Daisy's brown mongrel, which seemed to have been bitten by every dog on the street. Above the chest of drawers was a piece of glass on the wall which acted as a mirror, and adjacent to this were some unpainted shelves made from cheap rough board. The children had to pile everything on them or put their belongings in a corner or under the bed, or somebody would be stepping on them or threatening to throw them through the window. Above all, the water stained celotex presided, although sections of it had escaped from the nails and threatened to fall at any time.

The room she shared with her brother and sister was one of the two rooms which made up the small house. The other room was her mother's. It was just the same size as the children's but boasted a single bed, a dresser, a small table with four chairs, a colour television and a radio which were both placed on the table.

Thick ply board had been used to construct a small kitchen adjoining the children's room. In it was a small rusty refrigerator which was still working and a twenty inch gas stove, lately acquired. It added a kind of grand look to the kitchen and

6

seemed quite out of place with the rusty refrigerator and a wooden table which was used to store food items, pots, buckets and a sink basket with plates, cups and other kitchen wares. There were also several buckets of water and a big plastic bath sitting in different corners in the kitchen. There was no pipe or running water.

She was sitting in this corner now thinking about what she had heard. Her mother still did not believe that she had not chosen that exclusive upscale school. She did not believe when the teacher told her that it was her almost perfect scores which had earned her that privilege. She had gotten a perfect score in all but one subject – Social Studies. Everyone was happy for her. She had become the heroine at school and in her community. Everyone had called her wanting to congratulate and speak to her about everything and nothing in particular.

All her teachers from grade one to six said they were not in the least surprised and had expected nothing less, but her mother's behaviour puzzled her. At times she would look at her with such pride and awe which made her head feel as if it was a balloon being inflated. But the balloon lost air everytime her mother started complaining about the cost. Her mother also had another item on her list. One week after receiving the result, Martina was standing by the front door when she had the strange feeling that somebody was staring at her. She spun around to find her mother staring at her with a strange indescribable look on her face. Her mother continued to stare at her. She stared back, their eyes locked and Martina was the first to look away.

Her mother spoke at last. "I hope you don't t'ink you better dan everybody else jus' because you pass to go a big school or because you fa..."

She stopped immediately and walked away, leaving Martina thinking she had done something to offend her. What did she mean by her last unfinished sentence? Very often she made these unfinished sentences which made no sense to the child but caused her to think that her mother had something against her. This made her even more withdrawn.

For some reason she was apprehensive about going to the new school but she certainly did not want to go to Rockwell Comprehensive. She would tell her mother not to send her if it was going to be a problem. She hated causing problems and having everyone talking about her as if she was a pest which should be eradicated. She would stay at the school down the road and do whatever she had to without causing her mother to find money she did not have. She wished she could just disappear and stop being a problem or find a corner to hide in where no one could find her.

Martina opened her room door as quietly as she could and went through the kitchen door which had been secured by three large bolts. There were break-ins in the community from time to time and many people used similar big bolts to secure their doors. When she went through the door, she pushed it up and used a half concrete block to close it. She squeezed around the side of the house, almost touching the zinc fence that separated her home and the other house in the yard from the rest of houses.

The other house in the yard was much bigger than theirs. It had about five small rooms occupied by three families. There were about eight children, males and females ranging from toddlers to teenagers living in it. At the back was the one bathroom shared by the occupants of both houses. It had a shower and one had to stand on a piece of board in the little concrete square when bathing. There was an old, badly chipped toilet bowl, which was operated by pulling a chain which clanged loudly as if in objection whenever it was pulled. There was no face basin and the very hygienic had to wash their hands under the shower. Everyone had to take his or her toilet items to the bathroom. If one made the mistake of leaving any of this there, it would never be seen again. Martina hated this bathroom and avoided it when she could by bathing in the kitchen and pouring out the water on the gravel by the side of the house.

Someone was using the bathroom. There always seemed to be one of the sixteen people living in the two houses or their visiting friends and relatives using the bathroom. It was a very popular place in the yard.

She walked along the side of the larger house and went towards the front. Her mother hated when she went to the front so she sat at the side and for a while listened to the children playing, people swearing and cursing intermittently, boys hanging out on the street corner talking, laughing and playing dominoes or gambling and calling to every girl who passed by.

From where she sat, she could see most of the community of Dinsland, situated on the edge of the inner-city area. The community consisted of mostly very small houses like the one Martina's mother had rented. Some of the people had added to the houses rather haphazardly either by making additional concrete structures or using thick ply board or zinc sheets. Some people had also erected one or two bedroom plywood and zinc structures wherever there was a small piece of land available. This gave the community a very disorganized look with some houses standing directly behind others or others peeping over or hugging one another closely with barely enough space to breathe. However, some houses had a little breathing space, zinc or board fences had been constructed to effect a bit of privacy or establish boundaries.

Some people had also planted trees or a few green plants which chased away the drabness or created the impression of life attempting bravely to fight its way through harshness and squalor despite the inevitable. Some of the trees were fruit trees such as ackee, mango and almond, and when in fruition, formed part of the income of the people who lived on the premises — if the landlord did not come and gather the fruits before the tenants did — but the tenants often outwitted him. There were also the community leeches that lived by begging everything they could from both young and old. Not to be left out were the thieves who stripped the trees when the occupants were away.

Martina had lived at this place for almost twelve years. She knew no other home. The people, their way of life, their problems, their joys and sorrows as much as she could understand, were all part of her life. Her mother warned her not to get too entangled with matters that were not related to her or her family. She didn't have to try hard not to become involved as she was reading most of the times when the other children were playing games, simply talking, arguing or fighting. The children called her "Book head" or "Reada". She did not like the latter as it reminded her of an obeah woman she had read about. The woman was called a reada woman because she normally "read" or told her clients what was happening in their lives, especially who was trying to kill them.

She could hear some of the children playing now. They were across the street in Miss Dell's yard; Martina could hear her sister's voice above everyone else's. Yvette was very much her mother's daughter when it came to physical features, loudness and general mannerisms. She had the same fair complexion, frilly nostrils, brazen eyes and loud voice. She would have dressed as scantily as her mother did but for some unaccountable reason their mother did not allow any of her two girls to dress as if fabric was limited. While most females in the community, except for the Christians and Rastafarians, shamelessly exposed most of their bodies, Martina and Yvette had to wear 'decent clothes'. Their bellies, backs and most of their thighs were hidden; no shorts moulded their figures, no blouse shouted out what their bellies and backs looked like. Miss Fuller offered no explanation as to why she chose to dress differently from her daughters.

She sat on the stone for quite a while, sometimes listening to the noise around her, sometimes going off in a reverie about what her new life would be like if her mother found the means to send her to Milverton High. She wished she could go even to get away from her community for a few hours and to get away from her mother's strange, mysterious stares and partially finished sentences.

The sun was getting tired and pale after its long stint and twilight had come along to relieve it for a while before handing it over to the night and the moon. The children's voices had faded and Martina could see Yvette opening the gate. She pushed the gate harshly and it swung open making a loud, angry, grating sound. She came through and walked pass the front yard and along the side of the house towards Martina. When she was right beside her she stopped abruptly and said, "Tina gal you really weird! Why yuh sitting by yuh self a look in space?"

She shook her head and petitioned heaven for an answer. Getting none, she looked at Martina in a pathetic manner, still shaking her head. "You better come in now before Mammy start her noise."

Martina resignedly got up and went with her. Sometimes it made no sense to argue with Yvette.

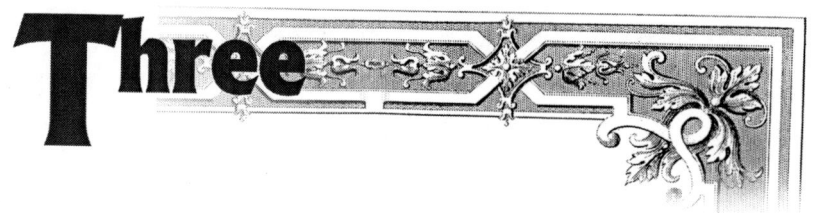

Three

"Good morning ladies and gentlemen of Milverton High School," said the principal, Mr. Tyrone Henning, with as pleasing a smile as he could summon on his broad mud-coloured face.

He was a man who height had snubbed, so his head barely rose above the podium. The notion that short people usually spoke loudly to make up for the lack of stature, ran true for Mr. Henning. His thunderous roar could be heard as far away as the school gate, which was many metres away.

"I welcome you heartily to Milverton High, especially the grade sevens who are here with us for the first time. You have no doubt worked extremely hard to pass your exam and I trust you will work even harder to maintain your place, and after five years graduate with excellent passes and as a human being who can relate to the rest of the world and make a worthwhile contribution to this world."

As he spoke Martina fixed her eyes on him. She was standing at the back of one of the grade seven lines. She did not want to stand at the front and have anyone take any special notice of her. She did not particularly like her shoes. They seemed flat, broad and inexpensive compared to some she had noticed before the bell rung. The girls all wore the same lilac uniform and the boys wore khaki pants with white short sleeve shirts. She was glad about the uniform as it made her inconspicuous; she wanted to be part of the crowd, not an individual. She felt shy and uncertain as if she had somehow been spirited into a strange land where she did not belong. This school was certainly quite different from her primary school, in fact everything seemed different, the community, the road leading to the school, the school's environment, the condition of the building, the very atmosphere, everything.

Her first sight of the community had caused her to spring instantly to her feet as if she had been bitten by an insect. She had been travelling on one of the large City Transit buses with her mother to Milverton to do her registration two weeks before the beginning of school. As the bus skilfully rounded the corner, tilted at a precarious angle and started to climb the hill, Martina was enveloped by a cool breeze which flowed down from the hill. There were huge beautiful houses sitting proudly with a lot of space all around; space for driveways and walkways, space for huge flower gardens, space for trees which grew without hugging one another; space for large swimming pools. These houses had individuality, an air of privacy and seemed to resent anything or anyone touching them. They could breathe freely, easily, without choking or gasping, unlike those in Martina's community. She had never seen anything like this before except on television and sometimes things on television were not real, but this was. Her eyes almost tumbled out of their sockets as she stared and her mouth gaped involuntarily.

She pressed her face on the bus window as it continued to ascend the hill. The further up it went the larger the houses became and commanded even more space. There were long lines of neatly groomed trees dressed in healthy green clothes and glimpses of extremely green lawns resting closely to the ground.

Having conquered the hill, the bus jerked to a stop and everyone got off. Looking straight ahead, Martina could see a high unfriendly looking gate with an even higher wall which enclosed the whole school compound and clearly showed that intruders were not welcome.

Martina walked in front of her mother and inwardly wished that she had not accompanied her. Already, her mother was receiving questioning stares from the people close by. Their eyes registered her orange wig which matched her loud orange and purple straight dress. The dress was little more than the length of a blouse and very clearly defined every curve and bulge in a provocative manner. Whenever she walked it threatened to reveal every fraction of her thigh. Her underwear escaped being an item on public display because of the orange tights she wore. High orange boots with orange and purple false nails and lipstick completed the outfit. Martina's heart sank into her soles. She wanted to be as far away as she could from this woman, especially when she noticed that no one else was dressed in this loud manner. The other women were quietly dressed in soft shades or earth colours and subtle floral. There was an expensive look about the linen and other material they wore. Her mother was clearly out of line, she had somehow mistaken the event or she simply just did not know how to dress.

After going through the school gate, the surroundings forced its compelling beauty before her eyes and she gazed about her, overwhelmed with wonder and reverence. Here again space reigned supreme. The buildings were well set back from driveways and the closely cropped sward edged by green plants, crotons, evergreen and other tall plants and trees. There were also well-arranged flower gardens with different shapes and luring fountains in the middle of some of the lawns. Martina wished she could curl up beneath one of the trees with a book and a refreshing drink of lemonade. The buildings were large, mostly two storeys with a gothic design. One got the impression that the architects had not merely designed a building but something special and different, something worthy of this upper class community.

She wandered away from her mother towards the side of the school and saw a glassy sheen barely shivering in the warm sunlight. She went towards it and discovered that it was a pool. A pool! She had never been near a pool in her entire life. She was enthralled at the idea of being so close to one and intensely hoped that she would be allowed to learn how to swim. She stood for a long while as if completely mesmerized, watching the water giggle when tickled by the wind. Soon other people came to look at the pool and she wandered back to her mother.

She stood in her line and tried to listen wholeheartedly to the principal but her eyes kept moving all around as she stared at the children and students whom she would have to live with daily. There was a strange unease mixed with a queer feeling of excitement that she could not define and quite involuntarily, questions sprang up at her. *What am I doing here? Will I be able to fit in? Will I make any friends? Will I be able to manage the work? Will my mother be able to find lunch money for me to come to school? Will the teachers like me?* Unbidden and fast, the questions assaulted her; some of them were like accusing persons pointing fingers at her. Involuntarily, she shrugged and blinked, refusing to face them.

The principal kept up his thunderous harangue and she tried to listen again but soon started observing the other students. True, they were all dressed in similar uniforms, but for people like her, the similarity in terms of belonging ended there. The shoes, hair accessories and watches of many of the students announced that they were from a different social background. These along with the look of intelligence and good breeding pushed her further into the background and again the question rushed to the fore of her mind.

What am I doing here?

She pushed it back and concentrated once again on the principal's speech but the girl in front of her stepped backward, almost crushing her right toes. She uttered a small cry of pain and the girl turned around, looked down at her feet and murmured a stony "sorry". After apologizing she returned to her former position but for some reason she spun around swiftly and looked down at Martina's shoes. The look did not end there but ended up with a survey of her uniform, watch-less left hand and stopped at her face for an uncomfortably long period. At first Martina stared back at her unflinching, and then when it seemed as if there would be no end to it, she blinked and looked away. When she looked ahead of her again, the girl had moved closer to the girl in front of her.

From what she had seen of her, Martina noticed that she was very fair, almost white, with short brownish hair cut close to her head and a nose that had started out being straight and then somewhere in the middle had flared out of proportion, ending up with broad frilly nostrils. A large number of students seemed to be of the girl's complexion. She had even noticed some who seemed to be white. The other students were a rich mix of varying shades of blackness although many would object to being called black because they were fair skinned.

The principal, by now, had finished his talk and the teachers and senior students saw to it that everyone marched off in single silent files to the classrooms.

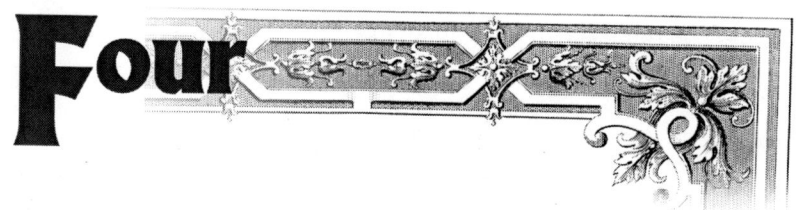

Four

Martina's classroom was large and spacious with a high white ceiling, large grey tiles and three ceiling fans. The desks were polished a soft shiny brown and the detached chairs were of the same material. There were shelves with green potted plants and rows of neatly arranged books. There were also two large cupboards which she suspected housed books and other learning materials. The walls were decorated with pictures and paintings of the school, the founders, national heroes and charts with lessons in different subject areas. In large flowery script directly over the chalkboard was the school's motto, "Excellence first and foremost". At the classroom door there was a large, clean garbage bin tightly fitted with a cover.

Martina chose a desk at the extreme back of the class that was right beside a window. Her classroom was upstairs and from her window, she had a vivid view of well kept lawns protected by avenues of green trees, cherries, pines, among others. She could also see one or two large houses and a block of buildings on the school compound.

She had no desire to sit at the front of the class and draw attention to herself. She watched silently as there was a scramble for the front seats. Even at this school students pushed and shoved vying for the front seats as if all the knowledge coming from the teachers would somehow stop there and refuse to go any further. Some students, after installing themselves in a seat, put their bags on the seat beside them, saving seats for their friends who were still trying to worm their way through the shoving and pushing. One girl almost fell, but held on tightly to the desk in front of her as if she had been cast into a raving sea and was holding on to a piece of wreckage to save her life. Martina watched, and though inwardly amused, not even a slight smile betrayed her amusement.

When the girl righted herself and sat in the seat, she turned around and stared savagely at the student she presumed to have pushed her. Martina's heart did a quick flip when she recognized the girl who had stonily scrutinized her at worship. *Why did she have to be in the same class as I was?* For some unknown reason, she felt a slight cold tremor race through her body and without realizing it, she shivered slightly. At that moment, she decided that she would keep out of her way because somehow she knew that any encounter with her would be less than comfortable.

The form teacher came in and everyone stood as if on one accord and chorused, "Good morning, Miss".

She wrote her name on the chalkboard and then said to the class, "My name is Miss Nolan and I will be your form teacher, your parent away from home for your stay in Grade Seven. I want you to know from now that we are a family and must treat each person as such. You must behave like brothers and sisters and treat one another with respect."

She spoke earnestly, her young, round, refreshing face expectant and eager. She was a tall, olive complexioned woman with shoulder length processed black hair. Her chest was flat and she had a place for buttocks but none was obvious. She seemed pleasant enough and Martina thought to herself *I like her, she seems friendly enough.*

Miss Nolan proceeded to read some rules for the class, after which she pasted a long sheet of paper with them on the wall. She then asked the students to stand and introduce themselves by telling their names, the school they were coming from and their career goal. The first person to stand was a white Australian girl. All eyes were riveted to her. Her name was Tarilla Hue. Beside her was Martina's stony 'friend'. Martina immediately dubbed her "Stone Cold". The girl sitting next to her she learnt was Pamela Prang. Ninety odd percent of her classmates were all coming from preparatory school and they all aspired to be top class professionals. Only three students, including Martina, were from primary schools and there were questioning looks on many faces when she named her primary school. It was as if nobody had ever heard of it. She received even more quizzical stares when she said she was not certain what career path she would follow.

The morning passed smoothly. They had two classes for the morning and were introduced to two more teachers, Mr. Light for Religious Education and Mrs. Pringle for Mathematics. Mr. Light's obvious mission at the school was to light the children's pathway with the shining light of God which shone through the words of love and encouragement he spoke to them. He obviously felt very deeply about teaching Religious Education because as he spoke his eyes lit up and his hands moved dramatically to emphasize his words.

Mr. Pringle, the Mathematics teacher, was quite a character. He was a healthy picture of a black man; tall, with a weight lifter's physique, a round glowing coffee coloured face with a thin nose and contrasting full lips. His voice demanded that you paid attention to what was being taught or there would be consequences. Mathematics was not necessarily Martina's favourite subject but the teacher's method of teaching compelled her to learn.

Then it was lunchtime, the harsh metallic clanging of the bell signalled it. To everyone, this was the most pleasant sound of the day; the sound which meant a brief respite from work and an opportunity to socialize. Now it was time for eating. Martina tried to make a decision about whether to take her bag along with her or not. She looked around and noticed that everyone seemed to be leaving theirs under the desk so she did the same. Underneath the desk was a good place to hide her bag which was made of cheap synthetic material unlike all the other brand name bags in the class. She pushed the bag under the desk and then made her way alone to the canteen.

In the canteen, students were talking and laughing as they waited in straight lines for their lunches. The prefects made certain that pushing and loud talking were minimal by threatening the students with detention. As she waited to be served, Martina looked around her. The canteen was definitely state of the art, spacious and airy with tiled floor and many ceiling fans. There were numerous drink machines all around which mocked the advice pasted on the front of the dining room that fruit juices were the best thing to drink any time of the day.

Martina ordered a patty and a small bottle drink. She had to be careful what she spent because her mother had warned her that the three hundred dollars she had given to her should serve her for the week for both lunch and bus fare. Already, she was thinking of the days when she wouldn't be able to attend school because she would have no money. Her mother did not have a regular job except for helping out on a Friday or Saturday in a dry goods store downtown. She considered herself above domestic work as she said, "Mi nuh want all kind a people who nuh better dan me tek liberty with me an' push mi aroun' an' use me fi dem gal!"

Martina wondered how she managed to survive on a one-day salary when she had three children to take care of. Only one of the fathers, not Martina's, ever visited or contributed anything to her welfare and this was very rare.

She was suddenly jolted out of her thoughts by a push from the girl behind her. "Missis if you don't move up how you expect us to get lunch?"

The push landed her right in the back of a boy who spun around quickly as if to rebuke her, but for some reason when he turned around and looked at her he merely hissed his teeth then turned around again. She was relieved not to be attacked from the back and front.

After receiving her lunch, she went and sat at one of the back tables trying to be as inconspicuous as possible. Soon she was joined by another girl and boy. When she looked at the boy she realized he was the same one she had been pushed into. He sat down without seeming to recognize her and started talking to the girl beside him. From the conversation Martina learnt that the names of the two were Tian and Miscah and that they were in grade nine. Their conversation was based mainly on an incident which had taken place earlier on in their class between two students.

"Angelique Belnavis really think she is something special!" remarked Tian with a scornful tone.

"Boy you can say that again! She thinks because somebody fool her that she is white that she is better than other people."

"Can you imagine she tell bright, bright Tenesha Bent that she could not sit down close to her because she too black!"

Tian was fair complexioned and as Miscah spoke his face became almost red with disbelief.

"Angelique Belnavis did so badly last year dat her mother had to beg the principal to make her repeat grade nine!" he continued.

"What, she repeat! Then why she showing off herself so! Before she try and see if she can catch something in her sieve brain!" Miscah exclaimed, speaking louder and louder.

"Sieve brain indeed! The bottom of the sieve drop out an' all that is left is a big hole. You know that we did story writing from grade eight already and this morning the new English teacher was revising the topic and ask her what is a plot. My dear, the girl tell her that it was a small piece of land for burying characters. The whole class burst out into one piece of uncontrollable laughter. Even Mrs. Dean had to laugh. See here, everybody was dying with laughter and when Miss told us to stop we couldn't stop, so she told us to stand up and threaten to make us stand up for the next period if we couldn't quiet down. So all the students put their hands over their mouths and tried hard to stop. But Ginette Burns she couldn't stop and all eye water was running down her face. Miss had to put her to stand at the back of the class and even then she was still laughing. Of course Michael Munroe, the class clown, right away nick-named her "Plot" and everybody started calling her that."

Miscah was laughing so much that she spilled some of her drink on her uniform and choked on her food. She had to run outside to the bathroom.

Even though she was pretending not to listen to the conversation, Martina could not help smiling. She kept her head down and pretended to be concentrating on her food.

"Are you a new student?" Tian asked.

At first she pretended not to hear him and concentrated on her food as if it was the single most important thing in the world but Tian repeated the question.

"Are you a new student?"

This time she looked up but did not look directly at him.

"Yes," she answered.

"What grade are you in?"

She glanced briefly at him before she slowly answered, "Grade seven."

"So how you like dis school?" he continued his questioning.

She thought to herself, *Why is this boy asking me so many questions. He is a policeman or what?*

He saw that she was hesitant to answer and repeated, "Do you like the place or what?"

"Well, I think it is big, clean and pretty," she answered, looking back down at her food.

"I hope you enjoy it here," he said.

He looked towards one of the canteen doors where Miscah was entering then he turned to look at her and said, "I caa put mi finger on it but you look like somebody ah know from somewhere. Right now I caa figure it out but something about you remind me of someone I..."

He stopped speaking because Miscah had come back and was pulling out her chair to sit down.

As she sat she said, "You know dat as soon as mi go into the bathroom two girls come and was talking about the same thing! Bwoy story can really fly fi true!" Miscah remarked.

The two started talking about track and field training and other school activities. In this way Martina learnt about some of the most popular students in the sporting area and that Tian himself was an athlete.

The bell put an end to their conversation. Martina rushed to the bathroom before she ran to her class. She marvelled at the cleanliness of the bathroom. It would really be something if she had a bathroom like this at home.

The remainder of the school day was uneventful except for a slight incident with Stone Cold. It was at the end of the school day and she was going down the stairs when she saw Stone Cold with three other girls. Already she had formed a gang consisting of four students. They stood by the side of the stairs and when they saw her coming they stretched their feet into the way. She nearly fell and as she staggered to stand upright one girl cried out, "My God, those shoes. Is must Belvin dump she raid! Anybody could sail to the end of world in that, good God."

Belvin dump was the city's main dump.

Martina felt her temper heating up. Her mouth started to tremble and the tears started to gather but she pushed them back. Involuntarily, a fist began to form. She did not speak but stepped over their feet, went down the stairs and through the school gate. As she walked away shouts of "Boat boot, boat boot" trailed her.

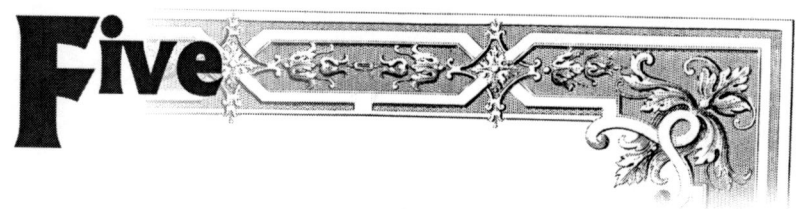

Five

Martina got off the bus stop closest to her home. She felt strange getting off the bus coming from school because when she was going to primary school all she did was walk the three blocks to her home. As she alighted, she saw Miss Myrtle who sold sweets, biscuits and cigarettes at the bus stop. Miss Myrtle was a woman who was physically well endowed at both front and back. Her huge breasts stood erect and pointed as if they were in malice with the rest of her body. Her huge stomach and buttocks joined in the disagreement by pushing themselves as far away from the rest of the body as they could. Whenever she spoke she did so as if the words were rushing from somewhere and she could not control the flow but had to say them very quickly.

"But Reada gal you stop go primary school now an' a go a secondary school. A since when dem change the uniform to that colour and where you coming from off dat bus you one?"

"Hi Miss Myrtle," Martina replied, pausing in front of her but soon had to move as there was not enough room for Miss Myrtle's body and hers on the sidewalk. She stood beside her and continued speaking. "I am not going to Rockwell Comprehensive, I go to Milverton High."

"Milverton High, which part in town you fine dat school and how come you lef all the way from down here to go there, who sen' you there?"

By this time she had turned to face Martina, and her huge belly pushed against her and she had to step backwards.

"That's where I pass the scholarship for so that's where I am going. The school is way up Milverton and I have to take two buses," Martina answered quickly, hoping that Miss Myrtle would go back to her selling.

There were two people waiting on her by now and they were listening to the conversation which made her even more uncomfortable.

"Milvaton! Then nuh rich brown and white people and bright pickney go to them kind a place so how you reach there?"

There was amazement and disbelief in her voice as she stared at Martina. Her breasts and her belly also moved closer to her.

"I am not rich, brown or white but I did pass the exam for there," Martina replied, slightly walking away.

"Well chile a hope you last up there cause a don't know where you mother a go get money from to sen' you up there, a wish you luck."

With this she turned to her customers and one of them said, "Bwoy she mus' a really bright to get to go that school. A hope she hold up her head."

Martina continued her journey trying to shut out the voices. She thought to herself, *How come everybody find it so strange that I am going to that school, I must be the first person from Dinsland to go to a school like that. It must be the ninth wonder of the world. And trust me I am going to make them all see that it was not a mistake.*

She quickened her step and turned into her lane. There were quite a few people on the road, in addition to children playing in the yards. Almost everybody turned to look at her, called to her or asked her some question or the other about the school she was attending. She tried to answer all the questions because if she did not it would be thought that she was proud and in the lane, that did not sit well with people. You would be directly encouraging harsh words and criticisms if you pretended that you were better off than anyone in the lane.

There were several groups of boys idling on the road as usual. Martina hated to pass them as they always made rude remarks about her getting big and consequently being ready for sexual activities. She hated the lewd words and suggestive looks and wished the boys would suddenly evaporate before she passed by.

They did not. One of them, puffing noisily on a ganja spliff, walked unsteadily out of his group and shouted to her, "You going a high school now. Go on for now cause a soon take you out a dah uniform deh!"

"Lef' the little gal alone Bull. You know that she a try. An' you know that her mother will chop you up! Easy you self nuh!" admonished Gerald, a tall, wiry, dark young man who was grinding something in a piece of brown paper.

Martina ran pass them and did not stop running until she was at her gate. Once inside, she closed it and tried to regain her composure. She hated them so! She hated this place and those boys who did nothing all day but prey on young girls! Why couldn't they be like Mrs. Lyttle's two sons who had finished school and were working and were never seen tormenting anyone on the street!

She called out to her mother to open the door but did not get any response; she walked over to Miss Turner to get the key because that was where her mother always left it when she was not at home. Martina wondered where her mother was. She only worked one day out of each week but many times she left the house saying she was going out. More than once Martina had peeped into her room late at night and she was not there. Where did she go? By the time she woke up in the morning she was there. She could never understand adults.

"Miss Turner, Miss Turner," she called as she walked to her front door.

"Is who that? Is you Tina?" Miss Turner enquired, peeping through her window.

"Yes, Miss Turner is me," said Martina. "Mummy leave the key here Miss?"

"Yes dear she say she have a little business to do so she gone down a town little bit." She opened the door and stood on one of the steps looking proudly at Martina with a smile on her face. "Girl, you look good. A proud of you! Oh God you really look good. How was school today?" Without waiting for an answer she continued, "Girl a beg you, work hard and hold up you head! Nuh look down. You will make it in this life if you look up! Forget grudgeful people and the ole tired bwoy dem and hold up your head."

"A will try hard Miss Turner, a will try hard," replied Martina in earnest. "Miss Turner, you see Yvette since evening?" she asked.

"No Tina. You don't memba that she doing extra lesson this year so she not coming early as usual."

"Oh yes, a didn't remember at all. And you don't see Shim at all either?"

"No. Him always take him time to reach home. A wonder what him do after school over from 12:30?"

"A don't know Miss Turner an' Mummy tired to talk to him but him don't listen."

"Well go in an' lock the door tight tight an' don't let nobody in!" she cautioned.

Martina left and did exactly as Miss Turner had said. She quickly changed her clothes and decided to bathe before anyone else came. She opened the back door, got some water from the pipe, poured it into the bath and then locked the door.

As she had her bath she wished that one day she could have a proper bathroom. What would it feel like to stretch out in a bath and allow the water to cover her? Water with soft, sweet scented bubbles like those people on television or those rich children at school had; water like that in the sea. Whenever she got the chance to go to the sea, she was always reluctant to get out of the water. It was so cool and soothing, and there was always a feeling of freedom. It never failed to exhilarate her. She was always in a good mood afterwards and often wished that she could be a mermaid or live close to the sea so that she could enjoy the water.

As if she was hit by a sudden revelation, she realized that there was a swimming pool at school. At that very moment she made up her mind to learn to swim and not just learn but to do well at it. Her grade six teacher from her primary school always told the class that if you wanted something badly enough and worked hard at it, then you would be successful. She resolved that she was going to take on swimming and excel at it. This was the sport that she was going to participate in of her own accord.

Just thinking about learning to swim almost made her push the unhappy episodes concerning her shoes from her mind. When she had gone with her mother to buy the shoes, her mother had told her how much money she had to spend and had warned her before she left home that if she wanted an expensive shoes then she would have to take her old bag to school or put her books into a scandal bag. She didn't want to take the old bag which had so many holes and reminded her of the sheet that she and her sister used to cover with when it became cold. At her old school it was not a problem because many children had bags with holes, but she certainly would be conspicuous at a school like Milverton High. She would prefer to take her books in her hand rather than take that bag. She knew the bag her mother had brought for her was an imitation brand name and she didn't really mind it at first because it was new but now all those wealthy children with their expensive bags made it seem as though learning and knowledge could be gained only by those who had expensive bags.

She was worried that because she was not rich or brown, many of the children would not want to be her friend. She had never been a very gregarious person but a few friends would do no harm. She didn't want to be an outcast. There must be some children who were like her who could be her friends whether she had a watch or a pair of expensive shoes or bag. She would certainly not go out of her way to make friends but she would not stop anyone being friends with her either.

At her old school she had a few friends but the number had been restricted on account of her not being interested in playing games but in reading all the books she could get her hands on. Her special friends were Gina and Patrina but she had not seen them since the holidays. They were both going to one of the high schools in the area. She missed them very much; if they were around she would not feel so lonely. She could not wait to see them to tell them about her new school, they would certainly be awed, but what would she tell them when they asked about new friends? Well it was still early; she still had time to make friends.

Her thoughts shifted to dinner as she was hungry but she would have to wait until her mother came and fixed the usual tin food, vegetables or chicken back. It was almost always the same with rice always present as if it was the weather. It was rice and chicken back, rice and tin mackerel, rice and corned beef, rice and callaloo, rice and this, rice and that. Ground provision was very rare and then this was only available on a few Saturdays when her mother cooked soup with chicken foot or soup (beef) bone. It would be very fitting if the whole family added rice before their Christian names. When Yvette's father came with a little money for her they always had a good dinner or sometimes when her mother came up with some money from somewhere. That was one thing that puzzled Martina, sometimes her mother would suddenly have extra money to spend. For example, a few months ago when she bought the new gas stove, Yvette's father had not come at that time and even if he had, he would never give her so much money for her mother to buy a new gas stove.

Her brother Shimron had exclaimed at the time, "Bwoy, new gas stove! Money a run! What a gwaan?"

His mother told him to mind his own business and try and pay attention in school so that he could buy one better than that in time. Shimron had responded, "Trus' me I will buy one better than dat an' I will buy even more."

His mother had looked at him and shaken her head. Shimron had been a cause for worry of late. The principal of his school had called his mother earlier that year and reported that he was too often absent and late, hid away from classes and did very little work. She had begged and admonished him to desist from these negative attitudes but he claimed they were not true and that the headmistress hated him because he was not bright nor told him things about other students. His report had proved him a liar and so had other people who had seen him at places where he should not have been. His mother had tried to beat him once but the ferocious, foul look on his face had deterred her. She had stepped away from him in shock and since then had resorted to cursing, threatening and making invocations of bad luck.

She had just finished bathing and putting on her clothes when she heard a knock at the door. She did not answer but went into her mother's room and peeped through the window. It was not her mother or siblings but Yvette's father. This was one of his rare visits. She hated when he came and her mother was not around. He was a big brown man with a flat nose and small eyes that dug deeply at you and made you feel uncomfortable. Martina definitely did not like him. She wished her mother was there or Yvette or Shimron. She wanted to pretend that no one was in but knew that her mother would never forgive her if she made him go away with the little money he always took for Yvette whenever he came to visit. She decided that she would talk to him outside, not in the house.

She opened the door and made to go out to him but he pushed pass her and stepped inside while she stood in the doorway.

"Where is you mother chile?" he asked, looking around as if he was seeing the contents of the room for the first time.

"She is not here," Martina answered.

"So where is Yvette?" he asked, coming further into the room, his deep eyes darting all around then coming to rest on Martina.

"She has extra lesson so she don't come yet. You can go down the school to her," Martina quickly added, hoping this would make him go.

"I will wait until she come," he answered, drawing closer to where Martina was standing. She quickly stepped through the front door and stood on the step. She didn't like this man or the way his eyes dug into her. She felt better outside. But instead of sitting down he came to the doorway and said, "Mi hear that you a go a big school. You turn big gal now."

Martina looked at him and said, "I am twelve years old. Two years older than your daughter."

"Yes but you look big for twelve."

He reached out as if to touch Martina but she recoiled and went down the steps and stood at the bottom.

He stood where he was and looked at her, his eyes burning boldly into hers. She averted her eyes and looked around, hoping that a member of her family would come. There were many things that she did not quite understand but her mother had told her to be careful of men and not let them get too 'bright' or 'touch her up' or else she would murder her and turn her out of the house. She didn't tell her what she was supposed to do if it was done against her will or if a family member or close family friend attempted to do it. Right now she knew that she was not going to go back into the house because she did not like the looks or behaviour of that man. But if her mother came and saw her standing outside and him inside she would think it was rude and would want to shout at her or hit her. She could never tell her that he had tried to touch her because she would accuse her of lying or plotting mischief against big people. She would also ask her what she meant by trying to touch her.

She went down to the bottom step and sat sideways, wondering what to do. At that moment she heard the ringing loud voice of Yvette and her friends coming down the lane. As they got closer she could hear most of the conversation or rather what Yvette was shouting at the others.

"My girl that deejay a fool. Him can't hot up t'ings like Mikjay! Him lyrics stupid and stale my girl!"

"But my girl all MikJay talk bout is girl and gun."

"But my girl is dat run the world. What else? Is better him talk bout what happening than a whole heap of foolishness."

The argument ended when they came to the gate and started walking through the gate. Yvette's friends had accompanied her home. Their homes were just down the lane about five or so houses away and since they always came to visit her, their mothers knew where they were and would often come down the lane and shout for them to come home.

"Hi Reada," she greeted her sister, heaving her overburdened bag from her back. "How come you sitting out here? God a come or fire inside! How you come so early from you new school?" She spoke as if Martina was far down the lane or locked inside the house.

"Hi Yvette, your father is inside," she told her without answering any of her questions.

"My father!" The response showed both surprise and fear.

"Yes your father and he is inside waiting for you," Martina replied coolly.

Yvette placed her bag on the step and peeped inside. Her father was still standing inside the doorway looking out at nothing in particular. He did not like the place but liked to think that he was a good father when he could find it in his heart to visit his daughter every month or so.

He had several children all over town and he really did not have the time to visit all of them regularly. His wife would object because she knew about his roving eyes and the many children he had all around the city. There were four of them about Yvette's age, all born within a month or two apart. His construction business did much better than he pretended but he always told the mothers of his kids that he didn't have any money, as there were many mouths to feed and bodies to wear clothes.

The little 'fowl feeding' he gave each mother could barely suffice for two weeks for one child and hardly for a week for mothers like Yvette's who had several children and used the money for the whole family instead of for one child. When she told him she needed more money he told her that he had fathered one child not three and was not going to assume other men's responsibility. He added that she should go and search for the other children's father and not try to use him because he was not born a fool neither was he born when his mother was learning her ABC. He had said some other rude things and had looked at her in such a despicable manner that she had shuddered inwardly and felt like a piece of dirty discarded rag.

This was the man who had promised to help her to start a small vending business in the commercial area downtown. As soon as she told him that she was pregnant he became as scarce as a public holiday. Initially, he told her to get rid of the child because he had fathered too many already and could not maintain another one. She refused and reminded him of his promise to give her a start in life but he measured some metres of hard-core indecent language and told her to get lost. It was only after taking him to the family court that he had reluctantly accepted his responsibility.

Yvette did not really like him because he spoke too harshly and was always threatening to beat her even though he did not live at her house or know anything much about her. She hated his sharp cutting eyes and never looked straight at him even when he commanded her to. She walked to the door and peeped in, not wanting to go in, as her mother was not home.

"Good evening," she said softly and shyly, quite unlike the Yvette that those accustomed to her knew.

She was like a subdued wildcat, which was about to be locked in a cage. She always said good morning or good evening, never adding 'daddy' or 'father' because she did not regard him as such. He felt rebuffed by this as if he could read the child's mind and knew what she was thinking. He always insisted, "Good morning, who?" but no matter what he said or how much he threatened her, Yvette, like a stubborn donkey, refused to budge. Eventually, he had given up, commenting loudly to no one in particular that some children simply did not have the right parents to bring them up and that was why young people were so ill-mannered and were giving the police so much trouble. Yvette's mother had been extremely tickled about this, she laughed loud and long beating the sides of her feet with her hands and shaking her head from side to side as if she was a battery operated toy. Finally she announced that "people who live inna glaas house should never fling stone at other people's place". Yvette's father had looked at her in such a manner that if he was Medusa she would immediately become stone.

After Yvette told him good evening he launched his usual caustic attack.

"What time is it now?" Without waiting for an answer he continued, "What you doing on the road till now? A sure school over long time so what you doing on the road so long, tell me dat little gal."

Fire had ignited fire, and Yvette retorted, "A start attending extra class for GSAT and everybody know that it don't finish until four o'clock."

"So you tek half an hour to walk from cross the road to down here! You mus' be related to snail!" Yvette did not answer but watched him like a cat eyeing a lizard ready to dash away if he showed any signs of grabbing her. He stayed where he was, watching her like a predator, a strange look in his eyes. "A hope all the money mi spending on you don't go to waste," he said. "You make sure you pass whatever SAT you doing or hell to pay!"

"Is what you threatening the chile for now. Every time you come you jus' a threaten, threaten the pickney so," said an irritated voice from the doorway.

They turned hastily around to see Yvette's mother standing arms akimbo on the top step. She flounced through the doorway, dropping a plastic bag that she was carrying on the bed.

"So where you coming from now?" asked Yvette's father in the same tone he had used earlier to address Yvette.

"But look here! Who you asking that question? I am my own big woman! I answer to no one but myself. Mi not your chile or woman, try memba that!" She levelled a scalding look at him but he remained undaunted.

"You don't work so why you walking street for? You suppose to be home when you pickney dem reach home," he rebuked her loudly.

"So where you are day an' night when your pickney dem go home? Where are you?"

"I am a man, I can be anywhere I want to anytime I want to so know yourself!" he flashed at her triumphantly.

They argued until a few people came out of their houses to peep. The argument ended when he threw down some dirty looking notes on the bed and departed, getting into his SUV and driving off speedily as if he was being chased.

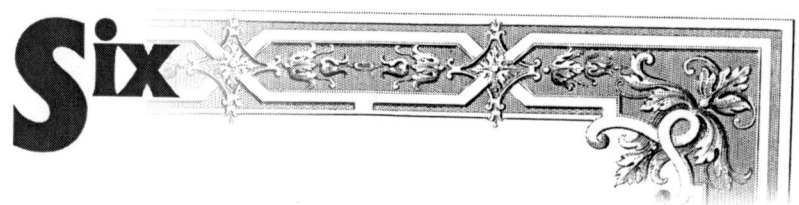

Six

School settled down to a routine after a few weeks or so. By now Martina had met all her class teachers and had tried to analyse them. She knew the strict ones who demanded much respect and hard work, and she knew the ones who you had to work hard for but could have a little fun at the same time. There were also about two teachers who thrived on making the children form opinions and draw conclusions from reading and allowing them to express their views within reasonable bounds. These were the English Literature and Guidance teachers. Martina found that Literature was as exciting as usual. Reading was her most favourite pastime and Literature her best subject.

Guidance was interesting too but she found that some of the views were different from the ones she was accustomed to in her community. The guidance teacher, Mrs. Prince, spoke about girls respecting their bodies and not having intercourse until they were married. Martina tried to count the married people she knew and ended up with a small number. Many of the people who had children were not married, her mother included, and she didn't think that this was so important. Look at her, she didn't even have a father, much less for him to be married to her mother; Shimron's father was nowhere around

45

and Yvette's father was already married. Moreover her mother had told her nothing of the sort and had only emphasized getting "something in the head" and earning her own money before she embarked on the maternal path. She didn't quite understand this marriage business and she didn't hear her friends and neighbours discussing anything much about it. When somebody in her lane got married it was normally an exciting affair with almost everyone lining the street to see the couple and comment on the bride's dress. A large number of them usually invited themselves, especially to the reception and created a food shortage.

Even though Martina was not knowledgeable about this topic she could not help thinking about many of the girls she knew who had started high school but did not finish. Many of them succumbed to pregnancy by grade nine, most of them by grade eleven. There was even a case of one girl who didn't even begin grade seven at all. That had caused her mother to get even more aggressive with her 'no man touching her sermons' but she had never told her about marriage. As a matter of fact, it seemed quite acceptable when the girls waited until after school to start relationships, as not many parents quarrelled then. The only other place she had heard a similar view to the Guidance Counsellor's was at church which she visited only a few times per year because she didn't have the right clothes to wear. Moreover, her mother did not seem to be too particular. It was Miss Turner who always invited the girls and insisted that they go because, as she told their mother, she was raising her children in the fear of the devil and not the fear of God. Martina thought those values were for Christians but here was Mrs. Prince reiterating them. It started to bother her and she thought that maybe it was mainly the rich, educated and fair-skinned people who did this. She was not of that ilk and moreover she was still very young so she would try and get something into her head so that she could get a job to help herself and her family. One day when she was older she would think about it some more.

Martina had, without meaning to, made two new friends. Mathematics was not her strongest subject but she had made up her mind to master it. Her Mathematics teacher was an excellent teacher who enjoyed teaching the subject. Martina soon forgot her mental block and got caught up in the subject. She found that she understood most of the principles being taught and the many ticks in her book testified to this.

One day in an Algebra class after she had worked out a problem and sat waiting for the teacher to come around to mark it, she noticed that Leonie Harris, who sat to her right, had only written the problem in her book and nothing more. She stared vacantly in front of her and seemed to have given up without trying. Without thinking, Martina leaned over to her and asked, "Don't you understand it?"

She shook her head, her plaits going from side to side as if to affirm her negative answer. Without waiting for her to ask for help, Martina proceeded to show her the steps in solving the problem. She didn't quite understand everything at first but by the time the teacher got to her she had worked out the problem. After school that day she asked Martina to assist her with her homework and she did. While she was helping her, she noticed that another student in the class was peeping over their shoulders trying to see what was going on. Every time she turned around he averted his eyes and stared straight in front of him. This time it was Leonie who asked him if he understood the homework and offered Martina's help without her permission. "Martina will show you how to do it."

At first he pretended to be just standing there, but he didn't move away either so Martina concluded that he was shy or maybe he didn't want the girls to think that as a boy he didn't understand when they did. He finally told them where he was having the problem and Martina showed him what to do. From that day on, the three would often do their Mathematics homework after class together. They also started to wait for one another at break time and lunchtime. The boy, Terence, 'Trace or Double T' as he was called, sometimes went to associate with his other male friends but Leonie and Martina always stayed together. Sometimes they even held hands when they were walking together. Leonie's mother was a teacher and transported her to and from school each day. Whenever Martina got to school before her she would wait by the school gate for her. After a while, Martina noticed that her mother did not take her to the school gate. One morning her curiosity nudged her to ask why this was so and she did.

"Leonie, why your mother have to drop you off so far from the gate and you have to walk so far?"

"You don't want to know the answer to that one, trust me," said Leonie shaking her head and giving a kind of snort.

"Of course I want to know! It's kind of strange!" exclaimed Martina.

"Well you know my mother is only a teacher and the salary is not plenty so we can't afford the brand name vehicle like the Honda or SUV and so on. Well you know that most of the children at this school have some very rich parents an' if your parents don't drive one of the cris car dem you don't really count in certain circles here! Well my brother get suspension las' year because one of the rich boys told him that if he was like him he would never make his parents drop him in that old Lada that look like something his mother steal from scrap heap or fight the chickens for. Well my brother give him one thump in his mouth and it turn out into one big fight and they were both suspended. Of course, both parents were called in and the principal said they both were wrong. You could see that the other boy's father did agree with him because my mother said you should have seen how he look at her like an object of poverty when he saw her going into the car after the meeting. Well from that my brother told my mother not to come up to the school gate and let him off so she just don't bother."

Martina's mouth fell half open through the whole revelation as if something was stuck in it and was preventing her from closing it.

"Well if that is the case," she said after Leonie had finished speaking, "what happen to the children like me who have no car and take the bus?"

"You don't really exist. You are the ones who some people ask how you get here! Ignorant people think you are asked to fill out how rich your family is on the form for GSAT!"

This sobered Martina a great deal, she didn't really know what to think. She didn't really exist because she had to take the bus! Well she would have to remain a phantom, a shadow among the living because she didn't even have a father much less for him to drive a car. Her mother was out of the question because all she probably knew about cars was that they moved on wheels and are driven on roads. She couldn't even afford a good pair of shoes much more a car! This place was really getting more and more confusing, too confusing; marriage and cars, what next?

Stone Cold had formed her gang of four and they tried to bully and dominate everyone else in the class, especially those they felt were too dark, too poor or who ignored them. Martina fell in all three groups and more than anyone else, was singled out for special individual treatment. As soon as a teacher was out of the classroom, Stone Cold would somehow manoeuvre any existing conversation to the subject of shoes and would blatantly profess that the biggest, ugliest shoes she had ever seen or imagined was to be found in their class. More than once she invited her classmates to take a look at Martina's boat shoes. Some of them would accept the invitation and try to peer at Martina's shoes which were tucked neatly in front of her as if trying to escape the taunting eyes of the students.

She was no angel, she had sprouted no wings nor did she possess any long white robe-like garments so she became very angry. It was very hard to quell the fiery spread of indignation that consumed her and threatened to make her grab Stone Cold and pound her until she felt some of the hurt and pain she was experiencing. But she held on, laboriously counting to the proverbial ten as she had been counselled by her class teacher.

Her mother and neighbour's voice weaved their way through her misery and cautioned her, "If you fight and dem send you home that is your business cause I not looking anywhere else to send you" – this was her mother.

"Reada, let them know that people like us have claas and can behave too. Let them know we can shine too" – this was Miss Turner.

She didn't know about the shining and the class but she was going to try and behave herself for as long as she could. She didn't promise anybody that she would try and behave forever, but she would try. Trying did not mean that she was going to sit back and not answer them, neither did it mean crying so that they could offer her a bottle or a pacifier. She merely looked at the group of scrutinizers and remarked coldly and boldly, "My brain is not in my shoes but in my head! I prefer to walk on my soles and not on my brain!"

The retort was so unexpected that the children just stared at her, unable to summon any words to hit back. Instead they moved back to their seats after observing the deadly cold look on her face. One boy, Georgionet Beacon who had been nicknamed 'Hairnet Deacon', stood up and applauded loud and long. As he did so he smiled and smiled as if that day was the last day smiling would be free and would attract a tax thereafter. Shouts from the gang of four for him to take off his mother's hairnet and sit down were ignored. His olive face sent signals of defiance to the four and even after he had ceased to smile he continued to stand.

Georgionet was teased everyday; as a matter of fact some people had forgotten his real name and only called him Hairnet Deacon. He suffered the same or even more than Martina did because of his ridiculous sounding name. Although most people teased him jokingly, the gang of four did it in a mean malicious manner, always making biting comments about him and his parents. Martina did not tease Georgionet. She had never been a teaser mainly because she hated the things that the person teased would hurl back at his or her tormentors; things about the anatomy and distasteful things about females that they had no control over.

She always felt like retaliating violently when anyone tried to embarrass her in that manner, so she had decided sometime ago, not to provoke such comments. In addition, now that she had become the centre of ridicule for the gang of four, she knew how sickening and sad and how much like an outcast one felt when being teased.

She liked her school but her own classmates were trying to make her hate it. She loved going to school but whenever she thought of her unpleasant classmates she wanted to be elsewhere even though she had made her up her mind to do well and make everyone proud of her. Martina's persecution caused her to plunge deeper into her school work and already she was getting good results. Her half term report was due and she was looking forward to seeing her mother's face when she viewed the eighties and nineties she had received in all the subjects except Art & Craft. She could manage craft if she was taught but art seemed liked an unattainable talent that had somehow missed her like how birds had missed teeth. She would never be able to draw; it was just not her forte. Everything she drew seemed as if they were attempted by a six year old learning how to hold a pencil. Already she had given up and told herself that she had to make up for the lack in other areas.

At the end of school that day, Martina made her way to the swimming pool. She wanted to learn how to swim well so that one day she would be a part of the school's swimming team. It was a dream that she would keep to herself. She didn't want to tell anyone and be ridiculed. Her class was not doing swimming that term but those who were interested in swimming could always go to the pool after school and sign up, and one of the two teachers or the seniors in charge would assist you. There were quite a number of students who were involved in this programme. To Martina's relief the gang of four was not involved. At least she could get some peace and enjoy her activity.

On the walls nearby, she could see pictures of the team swimming and information regarding the sports. She learnt that swimming was a competitive sport and was the act of propelling the body through water with arm and leg motion and without artificial aid. The techniques displayed showed the free style, which is the fastest stroke, and the backstroke, during which the swimmer lies on his back and kicks with his arms in a dorsal manner. The breast stroke showed the swimmer face down moving the arms simultaneously, forward and out, and the butterfly stroke showed a swimmer with her body lunging over the water as the arms moved forward quickly and together. Lastly there was the diagram of the sidestroke with the swimmer lying on the side of his body, alternately moving the arms forward and backward.

At the moment she was not interested in diving but she stared with interest at the divers leaping into the water hand or feet first in a combination of somersaults and twists.

Tian, the grade nine boy she had met at the beginning of the term, was a junior member of the swimming team. He had not forgotten Martina and greeted her with surprise when she went the second time.

"Hi, you interested in swimming or you just come to watch?" he asked jokingly.

"Well, actually I am interested. I cannot swim but I would like to learn," she replied urgently, her face expressing her willingness to learn.

"Well we are here to teach you three afternoons each week Tuesdays to Thursdays. You will learn if you pay attention and follow instructions," he told her while putting on his cap. "I only learnt since I came here and I am doing well. I only come two times a week because I have track practice as well. What I miss I make up for on a Saturday." His eyes were bright as he spoke dearly, showing his love for the sport.

Martina could understand his exuberance even though she had reached nowhere as yet.

After signing up, one of the instructors, Miss Hutchinson, spoke to the new comers.

"I welcome you all. In order to ensure that no accidents occur there are some rules that must be observed and I stress must be observed. No student, team member or otherwise, should enter the pool without a teacher or the lifeguard being present. There has never been an accident here and I intend on maintaining such a reputation."

She went on to emphasize the need for discipline. She defined discipline as the will and determination to do something and continue doing something even when things go wrong and you want to give up. She told those who had no discipline that swimming was not the sport for them and as a matter of fact, no sport wanted indisciplined people.

Already Martina had gone through the basics and was learning how to move her body through the water. At her swimming sessions she forgot about everything else, her home and her classmates' teasing, all that mattered was that she was learning and enjoying herself. The water was like comforting hands and she was often reluctant to get out after the hour was finished and often had to be called out after everyone else had gotten out.

One afternoon after leaving her swimming activity, Martina went to the bus stop as usual. There were a few students there talking, laughing, poking fun at one another, discussing school happenings and making noise generally. They were all older students so Martina stood a little apart from them. The younger students were often told not to be too bright with the older students as they were grubs and all grubs should know their place. Knowing one's place as a grub meant doing whatever the seniors demanded when there were no teachers around. Some of the first formers had suffered greatly as a result of this. Most of what the seniors demanded of them was quite ridiculous while some things were embarrassing and mean.

Take for example Kenrath McDonald who had been given one dollar by a senior and ordered to purchase chicken, rolls and a drink, and bring back the change. When he had pointed out to the senior that was impossible as he had only given him one dollar, the senior had called two others to look at the money. They told him if he did not know one hundred and fifty dollars from one dollar he was a dolt and had no right to be at their school but should have been sent to one for the mentally challenged. They also warned him that he would be severely punished if he did not come back with the lunch and the change. He returned with the lunch bought with his lunch money, so for that day he went hungry.

Living on the compound in the caretaker's small cottage was a middle age man that was mentally retarded. His mentality did not exceed that of a six year old. Whenever the children saw him they would ask him to say his ABC's or repeat his nursery rhyme in return for sweets. If he did as they asked and no sweets were forthcoming, he cried and vowed that he would tell his mother so that she would punish them. One of the traditions among the students was that anyone who defied a senior in any way or showed a negative attitude would be asked to read a letter to Virgil, the mentally challenged man. It was normally a love letter which in no uncertain terms expressed great undying love. No one, especially a boy, wanted to do this. Paul-Anthony Meade unluckily was the one chosen to read the love letter. He was accused of being a snob and in addition was said to need seasoning because he had refused several commands to fill a bottom-less cup with water and bow to the seniors and repeat the grubs' pledge.

One day during break, during the second week of school, a group of seniors had pounced on him and marched him off to the caretaker's cottage in search of Virgil. They called him out and presented him with sweets, circled him so that he could not run away and ordered Paul-Anthony to read the letter. At first he refused, but when he was told that they would hound him forever and do worse things to him, he complied.

In a wavering tearful voice he read, "Virgil my love I have been in love with you from the very first time I saw you. Your eyes are like magnet drawing my soul into yours and your lips are like a mellow mango, juicy and sweet."

The crowd which had gathered by now hooted and screamed with pleasure, knocking one another's backs or rocking to the ground in uncontrollable mirth. One boy almost wet his pants and had to speed to the bathroom.

Paul continued, "My love you are my ackee and salt fish. All the great Jamaican beauties such as Cindy Breakspeare and Lisa Hanna fade into comparison when compared to you. I will always love you. You are my first and last love..."

At that moment a booming voice interrupted, "What is the meaning of this gathering? What is happening here?"

The senior who was standing closest to Paul-Anthony grabbed the letter and ran. Everybody ran! In less than a minute the crowd had dispersed and the only one left standing at the scene of the declaration was Paul-Anthony, the Principal and Virgil. Virgil was loudly protesting that he would tell his mother that a boy had interfered with him and she was going to beat him. Poor Paul-Anthony.

Remembering all of this, Martina stood a respectable distance away pretending not to listen. As she stood there she was startled by the sharp, screeching brakes of a vehicle that stopped almost directly beside her. Frightened, she looked up to the angry tones of a man who wanted to know what she was doing at the bus stop when she was supposed to be waiting inside the school grounds.

"I beg your pardon," Martina said in amazement, looking at the man.

When she looked up, he met her eyes then hissed his teeth angrily and said, "I thought you were Triana. You looked just like her from across the road."

With that he reversed his silver Rav 4 and drove through the school gate. Martina stood in bewilderment and wondered what on earth that was all about.

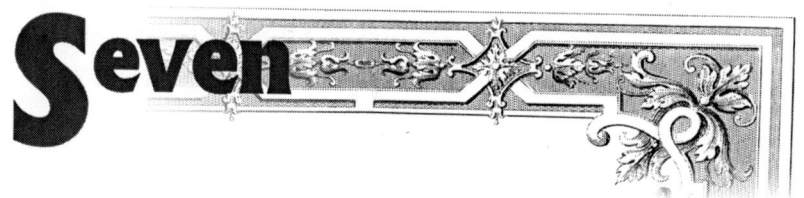

Seven

One afternoon at the end of the first term, Martina boarded the school bus at the school gate. She settled into a comfortable seat at the back and took out a novel. She enjoyed reading and did so whenever the slightest opportunity presented itself. Before she started reading, her eyes strayed outside and soon she got caught up in the scenery.

It was a grey afternoon; the sun had been subdued by dark ominous clouds which hung low to the earth. A fierce wind was blowing and the trees and other plants were bowing and dipping in an erratic manner as if they were being beaten and could not stand still. As she watched, a branch from a tree which was not able to fight the wind any longer gave way and with a loud cry fell to the sidewalk and partly on the road. The leaves, as if they were seeking freedom, tugged themselves free of the branches and went soaring into the air only to dive again, reminding Martina of butterflies at play. She wondered what weather condition had precipitated this and wished that she could get home safely before the rain made its appearance.

The Bryson High School for boys and the Ladies of the Convent School for girls were about two and three miles respectively from Milverton High once you descended the hill.

The bus had stopped several times to take up students from these two schools so the bus was almost packed to capacity and had become very noisy. The students were shouting, laughing, swapping titbits of gossip and courting. Many of them were behaving in a rowdy manner, ignoring the presence of the few adults who were travelling on the bus. The conductor appealed to them several times to tone down as they were not the only ones on the bus, but her request went unheeded as if she did not exist and was a mere shadow.

There was a big girl from Ladies of the Covenant High School sitting beside Martina. She had a CXC Biology text opened in her lap but her obvious interest was a sixth form footballer from Milverton High. The boy was dark complexioned and had an intelligent look. Two other girls also had the same centre of interest and they kept edging closer and closer to the boy who seemed oblivious of his magnetism. He stared through the bus window and did not even glance at either of them once.

A group of boys from Bryson High were standing behind Martina's seat. They were speaking in angry tones about an incident which had taken place at their school the previous afternoon involving themselves and other boys from a neighbouring high school who had travelled to their school.

"Trust me star my nine bills can't go like that. Watch mi, every cent of it a come straight back to mi." His voice swelled angrily and Martina could hear the quivering in it.

"But my youth why you give him the money before him deliver the goods?" asked the other boy with scorn and surprise.

"You see Lenford, is from last year we have this deal and him always play fair so I had no reason to think him would grab my money and run. When I get the phone me always give him to sell at his school and when him get phone me sell them at my school. After we sell them we always hand over the money and then I always give him a little tip too," explained the boy with emphasis, obviously trying to convince the other boy that he was no simpleton.

"Boy you see from I was a little boy, my brother and my friends tell me that I mustn't trus' nobody, nobody at all. When I bring my little weed to sell if a man not giving me the money same time 'im corner dark cause im not getting my goods! No money, no weed."

"Well it gone bad already and you never too old to learn so trust me, this is one lesson I learn and it will never happen again!"

He spoke vehemently, then seeming to realize that he was on public transportation, he lowered his voice a little but the resolve and fiery determination were still present.

"As a matter a fact if I don't catch him, boy from him school will pay, him going to sorry him cross me!"

"You think is a good idea to involve the other boys? How will that help you to get back your nine bills?" asked the other boy doubtfully.

"Well star me done work out everything already. Him have a friend at Milverton and Westmore and when me start deal with dem case a problem that. I man going to demand money from them and if them no give me, hell a go stir up. As a matter a fact if anyone of them set foot on this bus or let me see them, worries!"

His voice was as threatening and dangerous as the thunder that kept on muttering in the background. Martina had no doubt that he meant what he said. He was obviously involved in a dishonest scheme involving stealing and selling cell phones.

At her school several students who had left their cell phones in their bags or put them down carelessly had never seen them again. A few had also been taken from children's pockets. She wondered if the thefts were somehow connected as the boy had mentioned that his offender had friends at Milverton. She had heard stories in her community and on the news about schools feuding with one another. Some had started over girls, sports and sometimes over trivial matters. Many serious actions had resulted such as students being attacked and beaten, and one boy had been killed the year before when students had brought in a supporting gang from their community and they had stabbed an innocent boy to death. She hoped this would not happen at her school or anywhere else.

The primary school from which she was coming had not been involved in anything of the sort. Surely there were students who had taken knives and ice picks to school when they had disputes with others, but inter school warfare was new to her in terms of her school being involved. A sudden thought surfaced: *but weren't these schools located in so called up-scale residential areas and most of the students were supposed to be from good homes so why were they involved in dishonesty and fighting?*

From what she had often heard, inner-city children were the most vulgar and sinister beings, not to be trusted and often the ones who provided unwanted work for the police and were relentless in their efforts to bring the country to nought. Some people behaved as if children from the so called upper class areas had been decked out in purity from above and only occasionally fell. She was beginning to learn otherwise.

Her thoughts were invaded by rough voices, one protesting, the other accusing. While she had been engaged in serious reflection, the bus had stopped and had picked up a group of students. As soon as the boys had come on the bus the boy who had lost his nine hundred dollars touched his friend and told him that two of the boys, one from Milverton and the other from Westmore, were friends of the boy and he was going to confront them. The other boy told him to be careful because he would be outnumbered and more over the bus was packed. He also tried to reason with him by asking him how he could be sure that the other boys knew anything about the phone and the money. Well it would seem that anger was married to illogical thought because he pushed his friend aside and went and stood beside the boys who were at the back of the bus.

He stood there for a little while then he deliberately stepped on one of the boys' shoe. The boy spun around indignantly and said, "My youth, no earth could a soft like my foot so you must know that you step on me!"

"Idiot the bus pack and everybody is pushing gainst everybody so what's the big deal?" asked the offender staring at the boy in a nonchalant manner.

"The big deal is that you must feel you have stepped on me and you don't even say sorry and you don't look sorry either! Trust me my youth you begging trouble big time! You mother need to teach you manners."

"Mother, don't call my mother into this! I will teach you and your thiefing friends to have manners and not to trouble what don't belong to them!" he shouted into the boy's face defiantly.

"Is who this boy? Where you come from a call people thief? My youth which thiefing friend me have and who thief anything from you?"

The boy was truly incensed and one could see that very soon the verbal squabble would become a physical fight. A vein at the corner of his mouth was jumping furiously and his chest was visibly beating.

"Well, war declare my youth. Tell you thiefing friend Jerome say I send this present to him and I will send more until him pay my money."

With that he let loose a resounding slap across the boy's face. Simultaneously a loud roar of thunder announced itself followed by streaks of lightning zig zagging their way through the bus like a frightened person running through a maze or a crowd. Martina ducked her head quickly, not from the blows which both boys were now exchanging but from roars of thunder which now punctuated the blows that the boys were trading.

People were now screaming and trying to move away from the fight but they were barred by the fighters in the aisle. The boy whose friend had started the fight moved over and tried to pull them apart, but he received a thump in his belly which sent him tumbling in the other direction. He ended up in the lap of an irate gentleman who pushed him off roughly, swearing and cursing loudly as he did so. The boy staggered as he tried to regain his balance. As he did so indecent language gushed from his lips as if a main pipe attached inside had been broken and he could not control the flow.

As soon as he had righted himself by holding on to the bus rails, he went straight into the fight punching and hitting his friend's opponent. The boy who had been provoked and then attacked was now outnumbered two to one. His friends who had got on the bus with him decided to join the fray. Those who were sitting near by were treated to stray blows. Everyone was screaming and Martina pulled closer to the window. The bus started to rock dangerously and everyone was holding on to anyone or anything he or she could and screaming with all the effort that could be summoned. The driver seemed to be losing control of the bus as it started veering first to one side, then to the next. As the screaming rose to a deafening pitch, the driver managed to stop the bus but not before it slammed into the back of a Toyota Corolla station wagon taxi-cab that was parked on the right soft shoulder.

As the bus banged to a stop the passengers started dashing out in the rain that was now coming down with a vengeance. Some could not wait until those before them climbed outside so they went through the window. One very fat boy apparently forgetting his size, got stuck and started shouting for help.

Everybody was busy trying to get out so nobody paid him any attention. He shouted until he was hoarse, and as he shouted, the section of his body suspended outside was engaged in a feeble flying motion as one student later described it to another the following day. One woman wanted to know why anyone would attempt to swim in the air even though water was present.

After slamming into the car, the driver went outside to speak to the taxi-driver, who before examining the damage done to his car, had grabbed a machete from a coconut vendor close by and jumped into the bus from the back door. He was momentarily bewildered when he saw the boys who were still fighting, trading punches and kicks. He was so shocked that he forgot what his mission was. He announced that he was the police and was going to shoot them if they continued fighting. He used the machete to hit the bus door as he spoke. The boys obviously thought that a policeman was on the scene and stopped fighting at once. Even though they had been warned about being shot, all except one of them got up and dashed from the bus as if they really were chased by gunshots. They left some books and bags on the bus and one boy even left a foot of shoe in his wild dash.

By now the bus driver had come back on the bus and when he saw the man with the machete in his hand, he pulled his from under the seat. They regarded each other and then the bus driver spoke. "Big man I can explain everything," the driver said, appealing to the taxi-driver's sympathy. His clothes were wet and he was nervous and uncomfortably ready for action if the taxi-driver pounced.

"Yea but what bout my car big man, who is responsible? Who going to fix it? Your government, and what me suppose to do in the meantime?"

He was extremely agitated and was brandishing the machete as he spoke.

"Well I sure we can work out something me and you," said the driver.

"Well talk fast, I listening."

He leant against the bus seat hopeful for a solution. The bus driver started talking to the taxi-driver and while he was putting forward his plan, the conductor and two other conductors peeped into the bus. Seeing it was safe to enter, they did so. By now the fat boy had freed himself and had managed to jump down outside to much jeering and taunting.

The three conductors saw the boy lying on the floor and called out to him to get up. In response he opened his eyes a little and then closed them again. No amount of shaking or shouting worked, as the only sign that he was still alive was the heaving of his chest. They could see by the crest sown to his shirt pocket that he attended Milverton High. On examining, him, they realized he was badly beaten and from all indications, had been trampled. His face bore dirty shoe marks, bruises and his forehead and chin had blood on them.

The conductor of the ill-fated bus was just about to go outside to seek help when two policemen arrived. They were driving past and had seen the accident and wet students and people huddled together wherever they could, and had come to investigate. They pointed their guns at the two drivers and ordered them to drop the machetes. Both did so quickly. Then they saw the student lying as still as a piece of furniture on the floor and started asking questions. By this time, three more policemen had entered the bus. After assessing the situation, two of them lifted the boy outside and placed him in the back of one of the two jeeps that was parked outside and drove off. The jeep veered right and left, carving a path among the slow moving vehicles, which were struggling to stay on the road in the pelting rain. The loud shrieking sirens insisted on the urgency of them moving aside so that they could get to the hospital in time.

Martina stood huddling uncomfortably under the dirty tarpaulin the coconut vendor had erected. She was trying to rehearse the events in her mind but the picture of the policemen carrying the injured boy to their vehicle kept impeding. It would appear as if he was dead or close to death. Rumours had quickly circulated that he was a Milverton boy and was not expected to live. She felt sad and bewildered and wondered which aspect of the incident was real and which was fantasy. No one would believe that she had seen and heard so much. It wasn't the fact that they had fought that weighed so badly on her mind as she had witnessed quite a few fights in the lane and outside her former school gate; it was the fact that she had not expected boys from the upper ladder of society to behave as they had done. She had always heard the declaration, "a ghetto dem come from, they can't do better". So where did these boys fit in? She wondered if they were from the inner-city, like she was. Everyone had been so surprised that she was going to a school regarded as being upper class, but where was the upper class behaviour and ideals?

That night she watched the prime time news, as she did most of the time, and saw the bus and the taxi which had been involved in the accident. The bus driver and the conductor had been interviewed and they gave their version of the fight on the bus and the ensuing accident. Some students were also interviewed and they gave their views of school feuds and how they could be stopped. The gravest moment came when the newscaster gave details of the injured boy's condition. He had suffered broken ribs and severe blows to the head and was slated to do an operation the next day.

The next day at school was a glum one. The teachers and classmates of the injured boy felt especially bruised and wronged about the incident. The boy's personality, academics, athletic prowess, positive alignment to Christianity, healthy social behaviour and all his attributes worthy of emulation sprung from the lips of many. It was as if he was dead and ideas were being colleted for his glowing eulogy. Only his close friend whispered about his known involvement with ganja smoking and stealing cellular phones. When his parents came to the school and spoke to them, genuinely trying to find out if he was in any way involved in undesirable behaviour, they added their lines of praises to the shining eulogy already written by the majority of the school community. The principal in his investigation unearthed no decayed corpses in dark places. The boy had somehow managed to elude suspicion and detection among everyone except those in his circle.

Martina listened to the conversation all around her; she heard so many versions of the fight that she wondered if it was the same one she had witnessed on the bus. The number of boys involved in the fight had been added to significantly, the blows administered had taken on movie-like proportions and the injuries as described by many could not fail to prepare him for the eulogy already verbally written. She told what she had seen and heard only to her friends Leonie and Terrence. They looked at her with unmasked envy as they wished they had been the ones to have heard and seen all that had transpired.

The incident on the bus was the beginning of a school feud between Milverton High and Bryson High. Students made certain that they travelled in groups whenever they took the bus or went anywhere in their uniforms. The boys detached their crests from their shirt pockets and started using pins to attach them during school hours. They disappeared completely as soon as they went through the school gate. Extra curricular activities were completed earlier than usual as students were afraid of travelling in the late afternoon on public transport. Those whose parents collected them at school did not have the problems that those who commuted did.

The students who took the bus were often engaged in verbal war-fare and near fights and beatings. Since Milverton High was the last school on the bus route, they were in more danger. The drivers started taking mostly the Milverton students and leaving the Bryson High students behind. They were only allowed to travel on the buses most of the time if the buses had stopped for adults and they pushed themselves in. The robot taxis did a thriving business and in many instances overcharged students, who complained but still paid as they wanted to arrive at school. The public shouted foul because it claimed that Milverton students were being favoured, and if the buses did not want to take one set, they should not take the other. The drivers ignored the comments on the pretext that they were trying to prevent further clashes and possible loss of life.

Martina's mother warned her not to stay over after school but she was entirely committed to her swimming and did not want to miss any of the sessions so she did not heed the warning. She reasoned that swimming was only one hour for her group and that at the time when she left school there were many students at the bus stop so she was not alone. She did not tell her mother about her experience on the bus except that there had been a fight and they changed buses in the lashing rain and that was why she had arrived home so wet and dishevelled.

The injured boy did not return to school until one month later. He was treated as one who was returning from war and had performed noble deeds. He had lost weight and walked with a pronounced limp, bearing down heavily on his left foot. He was very subdued and reminded those who knew him of a sunny sky that had been overpowered by scowling clouds.

Eight

It was a Friday night. Friday nights were known as Reggae Friday in Martina's lane. From as early as five o'clock Turbulent Disco invaded the neighbourhood with loud bellowing music which usually rose to a screaming pitch by midnight. The music rode the air, blocking out all other sounds. It welcomed you as soon as you got off the bus, walked with you to your place of abode, accompanied you as you did your chores, followed you to the bathroom, ate with you and intruded in your private conversation. It was a constant unwanted company that refused to go away however much you tried to ignore it. In the late afternoon into evening and a part of the night, love songs, rock steady and light reggae from the sixties onwards dominated. After eleven, one's hearing and sense of decency were assaulted not just by loud, lewd dance-hall lyrics but by a deejay who interrupted almost every line of the song in order to scream obscenities, affirmation of what was being sung and played – indecent verbal games which poked fun at the anatomy and relationships.

It did not seem to matter to the lovers of these sessions that even though it was supposed to be late night or early morning, many children were still awake or could not sleep soundly because of the loudness of the music. Many of the children in the lane were able to sing or chant verbatim every word of these songs much to the embarrassment of many adults. They sang or chanted them in groups, over chores and used them even at play. Many of them were not even conscious of what there singing or chanting, but did so none the less because the pulsating, compelling rhythm of the reggae beat wafted its way into their ears and into their souls. It was part of the culture of the community and those who had grown up there would have considered it black Friday if the music was missing. Appeals made to lower the volume were often greeted with slight condescension or a barrage of expletives and threats. The police were not often welcomed by people in the lane so they were not called in. The music was just something you had to live with, a part of the air that you breathe.

The end of year examinations were coming and Martina was trying to study. It was not an easy task to study everything from September to June but she felt she had to as she did not intend to place anywhere but the first ten in her class. This was going to be difficult because the competition was keen and most students seemed to have a similar ambition where this was concerned. Stone Cold, though very mean, was a brilliant girl. She had gotten excellent grades so far and had announced to the class at large that she was going to be in the first five. Well Martina had no intention of being far behind. Her mother, Miss Turner and all the persons her mother had shown her half term report, end of term and mid-year marks, were all pleased that the sacrifice her mother was making was not in vain. Her grades were mostly in the eighties and a few nineties. The art of Art continued to evade her and her mid-year examination grade in that had been forty percent. She had placed sixth in a class of thirty-five and she was proud even though she secretly aspired to someday attain the number one position.

She had slept earlier in order to revive herself for the studying she had intended to do later on. Yvette was fast asleep in the bed beside her. She could sleep through any thunder and earthquake and if it was humanly possible, through the second coming of the Lord. If you woke Yvette to open the door for anyone in the house she would stagger to the door and go straight back to bed without even touching the door. If a moment of crisis arose which depended on her waking up or trying to save herself, it was only divine intervention that would save her. She always muttered incomprehensible things in her sleep and kicked around as if she was aiming at someone. She had done no less that night so Martina ended up on the floor in her favourite corner and tried to study but could not assimilate much because of the deafening music.

She put down her books and went into the kitchen to drink some water. As she passed her brother's bed the emptiness reinforced itself, Shimron had not come home and it was after twelve. Her mother had warned him not to leave the house at all but as soon as she had left after seven o'clock, he went straight through the door with a pair of his mother's drop earrings dangling in his ears. He was wearing his newest pair of Rocawear jeans and tee-shirt bearing the Member of Parliament's name at the front and the slogan 'I can make things right' at the back.

Martina loved her brother and they had a great relationship most of the time, but lately he had become a very closed person, refusing to look directly at her, speak jokingly to her, or tell her that she has to learn for all of them. She shared her mother's fear and worried about him and wondered what he did all day when he did not go to school or during the nights when he left the house right after their mother did.

Her mother too was a grave cause for concern. She always went out without telling anyone where she was going. At the moment she was not in her room, and already it was after twelve. Where was she? She had promised as usual to murder the girls if they ever put their feet outdoors. She always told them to lock the door securely behind her. She did not allow them to go to dance sessions. If there was an ordinary event or fair then she would send them, but dance sessions, no. Occasionally she would go to dances but she did not allow them to go.

As she stood there musing, she heard some shouts that seemed to be coming from close to her house, somewhere in the yard. She listened keenly but because of the screaming music she could not be certain so she went back to her work. As she sat down, the music stopped momentarily and she heard loud excited talking and shouting. One word detached itself from all the others and caused her to run to the window in her mother's room to confirm what she had heard.

As she opened the window, she heard shouts of, "Fire, fire down the lane! Lawd God fire!"

Martina rushed to the door and flung it open. She walked down the steps and then ran to the gate; sure enough there was fire down the lane.

She ran inside and tried to wake up Yvette who stretched and muttered and then settled back into a comfortable sleeping position. Martina tried again by hitting her on the hand. This time she got up, opened her eyes and declared that she didn't want to go to sleep that day until the next. She lay down again and then Martina resorted to the solution that always worked. She went to the kitchen and came back with some water in a cup which she sprinkled on her. She jumped up fully awake and angry, demanding to know why people could not sleep in their bed in peace. Martina shouted one word at her, fire.

She jumped up and shouted, "Jesus, you was going to let it burn me up!"

Yvette jumped up quickly as if she had been pushed from the bed and quickly put on the dress that she had been wearing before she went to bed.

"Lord Jesus, come quick nuh Reada. A want to see who house a burn. A wonder a what happen?"

Martina shook her head and said, "Yvette is me waiting on you or what? Really now!"

She quickly locked up the house and held the key tightly in her hand. Miss Turner's house was open and she came outside and locked the door.

Martina called to her, "Miss Turner, Miss Turner, Lord God whose house a burn?"

"I don't know but I aim to find out," Miss Turner replied.

They went out on the road hastily and joined the other people who were either walking fast or running down the road. Everyone was talking excitedly, speculating about the ownership of the house and the cause of the fire. The road was filled with people and Martina noticed that some of the females were still attired in their nighties. Some of the men and boys still wore their shorts they had worn to bed.

As they drew nearer somebody shouted, "Kiss me neck back is Julie house and her three pickney dem suppose to be in there!"

"Julie! But me see her up a dance nuh too long ago. She was a dance with Cutty her las' baby father."

When they arrived at the scene, Martina saw that it was indeed Julie's house. She knew Julie well enough. She was about her mother's age and had five children. Two of them were attending secondary school, but the smaller of the two was pregnant and she was only in grade nine. The other three were boys aged five to ten and attended the same primary and basic schools Martina had attended.

She had to push and manoeuvre her way through the crowd as if she was driving a vehicle on a crowded road in order to get through to the front where she could see. Yvette was right beside her. She had held on tightly to her hand as she wriggled and pushed her way through.

She could now see the fire clearly. Julie's house was a two room board structure with glass windows at the front and board windows at the back. The fire had completely taken hold of the back section of the house. The flames were trying to outdo one another as they leapt in high bounds reaching for the sky as if they were competing to see which flame could get there first. They were adorned in yellow and orange and chattered and groaned loudly as they pushed their way upwards. Their sharp sounds were even louder than those of the frightened people who were screaming and shouting.

Some people were asking the question that Martina refused to voice even to Yvette, where were the children? It was public knowledge that Julie did not ever take them to dance with her, but usually locked them inside. She always waited until they were asleep and sometimes the two youngest ones didn't even know that she had left the house at all, but the oldest boy sometimes got up and peeped through one of the front windows. The attire and the conversation of the session goers always attracted his attention. The females in their brief shorts, body hugging pants, almost bare tops and mini dresses, and the males in their shorts or full loose jeans and mesh merinos, tee-shirts and basketball jerseys always provided entertainment for him. They lured him to the window many times as soon as his mother left, thinking they were all asleep.

Somebody close to her said, "Somebody in the house trying to save them but him gone in there long time now an' him don't come out. Jesus mercy a wonder if him dead in there? The fire coming fast to the front now and him still in there!"

"But is who gone in there?" asked a scared sounding voice.

There was no response to this so the question travelled around the crowd and then from somewhere the answer surfaced as one woman bawled out, "Dem sey is Opposite the Rasta man from cross the road."

"Opposite, how that? No him get big lick on one of him foot dem and a hop and draw bout the place. What him gone in there a look for?"

As if in response to the question, a young Rastafarian man with his head held down kicked his way through the front door. He was half dragging a child as he limped out. A number of people rushed forward to him. They took the child and shouted for everyone to clear the way so they could find a place to put him.

Somebody shouted, "Call Round the World mek him carry him to the hospital."

Two persons ran off.

"But which part the other two little boys deh Opposite?" somebody inquired. "You don't see them?"

Other voices picked up the question and hurled it at Opposite. He was breathing hard and it seemed he could hardly speak.

He said in a sad voice, looking at no one in particular, "The fire was too big roun' the back and I and I could not go roun' there, is when I man almost did drop over something I see this one lying on the floor like him dead."

Before the words were properly out of his mouth some people nearby started bawling. One woman was so completely overcome with grief that she flung her hands into the air and then fainted, falling heavily and suddenly on two people who were standing beside her. A loud wailing rose up, which as if it had been planned, blended into the sound of the fire engine which hurtled into the lane and tore towards the fire with its siren screaming urgently and continuously.

The firemen alighted hastily from the truck, one almost falling to the ground, and started pulling out the hoses. Many of the men in the community rushed forward and started helping them. When the fire had been subdued and only feeble tired lines of smoke curled into the air, a large number of people tried to dash into what was left of the house. At their approach there was a loud tearing sound as the back collapsed. Everyone rushed back, almost pushing some to the ground. Some even fell over in the frightened retreat. They recovered quickly and rushed home or to nearby houses for tools to clear away the debris. Martina pulled Yvette away as soon as she saw two men emerging from the rubble with something in their hands. She pulled Yvette and ran straight home, crying as she did.

When she got home her mother was standing at the gate talking to some other people, she did not ask them why they were outdoors but took one look at their faces and told them to go to bed. The girls obeyed, but could not sleep. They laid in the darkness, a strange undefined feeling hovering around them. Although it was a hot night because summer was here, Martina felt a strange coldness walking over her body. She shivered and took up the sheet and covered herself. Snuggled under the sheet, the horror of the fire confronted her. All the details rushed at her, overwhelming her with the fact that it was just that luck was on her side why they did not have something unfortunate happening to them in the absence of their mother. She often went away leaving them on their own. The only thing was that they always knew where the spare key was kept and could get out in case they had to.

She heard her mother going into her room and after moving around for awhile, there was silence inside. Outside, angry, sad and bewildered voices went to and fro and she could hear them clearly. Something seemed to be missing but Martina could not tell what it was. Then it slowly struck her that the music had stopped playing. In the lane this was as strange as a week passing by without gunshots being heard. The music went on until five or five-thirty, you went to bed with it and woke with it.

Again she wondered where her brother could be. She had not seen him at the fire even though he could have been there without her seeing him. She had a feeling that he had not been there because he wasn't at home when they were alerted to the fire. All kinds of possibility flashed through her mind as she tried to imagine where he could be. It was the first time that he was staying out so late. Her mother, even though she could not beat him, would surely have some searing words to burn him when he eventually came home. She was not looking forward to the clash between them. Sometimes when she wanted to study, the problems always presented themselves and she really had to be determined and fight hard to keep them away. She fell asleep thinking about Shimron and his whereabouts.

She woke up suddenly to the sound of angry voices. All that had happened at the terrible fire forced themselves to her mind and for awhile she thought it was happening all over again. Sitting up in the bed, she realized that the sound was not coming from outside but inside her mother's room. She had no idea when Shimron had come in as she had somehow managed to fall asleep. The very thing she had been afraid of was happening. Shimron and her mother were engaged in a loud verbal battle of abuse, blame and threats.

"I can't help roaming the road all day and night, that is the example you set for mi, so is dat I follow," retorted Shimron.

"Yuh lucky dat yuh have me. I have to be both mother and father to all a you an' if it wasn't for mi you wouldn't even be alive," replied his mother.

"Yuh shouldn't have me den, is as simple as dat."

Martina covered her ears for a little while, hoping that her neighbours and passers-by would do the same. She did not like when people stared at her in a pathetic manner, wordlessly voicing their opinions of the family and their situation even though many of them were in similar situations. There were some who also seemed comforted by the thought that they were not alone and chastised themselves less.

Martina removed her hand from over her ears in time to hear her mother shout, "I don't want to hear anymore of your freshness. Get out of mi room."

She must have thrown some object which had found its target because she heard him cry out in instant sudden pain. She jumped from the bed and was in time to see when he grabbed her and started hitting her. Martina started screaming and crying. She rushed up to both of them and tried to pull her mother away, shouting at her to stop, but it was if she was a fly which had alighted on an inanimate object as her mother did not even look around at her. Her mother and brother were up against the wall when Yvette who had been awakened by the noise and the screaming, started shouting, "Police! Fire! Police! Fire!"

The word police somehow dragged Shimron to his senses and he quickly let go and walked to the room he shared with his sisters. He sat on the bed and held his head in his hands. He did not look or attempt to speak to anyone. Martina thought it was best not to go near him or speak to him. Her mother was sitting on the bed crying loudly, she had ignored the loud knocks on the door and the neighbours' query of what was happening inside. Martina could hear Miss Turner's voice above the others calling her mother and asking what was wrong. She wanted to let her in but she did not want the others to come inside so she shouted out to Miss Turner to go around the back. She opened the door and when she came in she locked the door behind her. Miss Turner walked straight into her mother's room and called to Martina's mother.

"Fuller is what kind a disgrace this big Saturday morning. The police jus' gone with Julie and you want them come back and take you too. Is what happen in here?"

Miss Fuller did not answer for a while; she kept her head down and continued to cry, sometimes softly and then loudly as if she was a motor vehicle which had been given more gas. The starts and stops continued for a while and then there was quietness. Miss Turner sat on the bed beside her and did not say anything until she had composed herself.

Then she said, "Is you and Shim quarrelling again? But why you don't leave that bwoy and let him continue him stupidness and when him get into trouble, him will stop give trouble!"

"Yes that's what all a you want to see, me in prison. But trust mi when I go there somebody else will be there with me or be in the hospital!"

Shimron rose from the bed, hissed his teeth, uttered a number of expletives, put on his hat, opened the door and then slammed it shut. There was a loud creaking sound as the door protested in pain and the little house shuddered.

Martina's mother lifted her face at last and Miss Turner saw a half swollen, slightly blackened left eye and several scratches on both sides of her face. The very short blouse which had not quite covered her belly was partially torn, revealing her black brassiere. She did not seem to care that Miss Turner was looking at her with reproving eyes as if she was a child in trouble.

"But Fuller, you need to look after you eye. You can't just sit down with it so! Is your eye you know and eye delicate, them don't make parts for dem! Reada bring some water in a basin and put some salt and dettol in it!" she shouted to Martina who was standing in the doorway with Yvette beside her.

Martina went into the kitchen and quickly brought back what she had asked for. Miss Turner took the basin and proceeded to wash the eye, talking angrily at the same time.

"Any pickney that don't have manners an' back answer them parents and worse quarrel an' fight with them must come to nothing. I live out more than half my days already and I see that too much time. Any pickney at all whether them right or wrong must have respect for parents, even if the parents do something wrong!"

She said this emphatically and looked meaningfully at Yvette and Martina to ascertain that they had received the message clearly. They looked at her face then looked away.

Miss Turner continued, "We are living in the last and serious days of time and children are surely wicked. The devil is their teacher and fren! When I was a girl no pickney could even talk hard to big people much less to quarrel and fight them. If you ever do that you know that your day is at hand, might as well you just drop dead and done!"

Martina listened and wondered what was the punishment for the adults who were not very good parents and who had adopted a lifestyle which said 'Do as you are told and not what you see me do'. Certainly Shimron had no right to quarrel and fight with their mother but if she stayed home some more he certainly would not find time to go on the street so often. After all, they didn't have any other adult around and since that was not the children's fault, Martina felt her mother should spend more time with them. She felt concerned about herself but felt that Yvette needed her more even though she had a father who peeped in on her occasionally. Yvette was too loud and sometimes vulgar. She was too spirited and needed to talk less. She would certainly get herself into trouble if more attention was not paid to her upbringing. Not allowing them to go certain places and forbidding them to wear revealing clothing were not enough. Her mother needed to change.

In a strange way, Martina felt sorry for her because despite her wandering feet, she still cared for them in her own way. She was not openly affectionate but she was savagely protective of her children and could not bear the thought of anything happening to them, or anyone interfering with them. As the boy in the street had said "she would kill you for her children". Martina knew that it was difficult for her to maintain her children with such limited finances. Her little job was nothing to speak of and with three children to school, it was very difficult. Once or twice she had gone to school with only her bus fare but she told no one.

Yes, things were difficult indeed and Martina wished there was someone to help. Even though she tried not to, she wondered who her father was. What was his name? Where did he live or was he alive at all? She had told anyone who had asked her, that her father was dead and that he had died since she was a baby. She wondered if he ever thought of her or even knew about her. From she had been in control of her mental faculties she had never seen a man living in their house. The only occasional male visitors they had over were a few relatives, Yvette's father and members of the community who stopped by to speak to her mother. Miss Fuller did not seem to have too much to do with the men in her community except to talk to them cordially for a few minutes. Her best friend was Miss Turner.

Shimron did not come back until the next day after his mother had left for work. She wore a pair of dark glasses and looked very subdued. When she walked up the lane she looked neither to the right nor the left and barely opened her mouth to greet those she passed along the way. Shimron said nothing to his sisters when he came in. He went to his side of the room, took off his sneakers and flung himself down on his bed and turned his back to the girls. His clothes looked dirty and his sneakers had a pungent odour. Martina did not know what to say to him and she was certain he would not respond, so she left him alone and went into her mother's room to continue her studying.

Nine

The new term had already started and Martina was now in grade eight. She was placed in the top grade eight class, 8m. In order to qualify for this stream each child had to be in the first five in the past end of year examinations. Martina had come fourth in her class and so had earned this place.

Her mother was very proud and had come the closest to smiling that Martina had observed since she had been in the fight with Shimron. The grades had been in the eighties and nineties except for Art & Craft, again. She had attained sixty eight in this subject and suspected that it was the theoretical aspect of the subject which had accounted for this. Her mother and Miss Turner, even though they had attained a minimal level of literacy and numeracy, understood the competition that Martina was up against. For a child to access grades in the eighties and nineties and come only fourth then it meant that the children involved were brilliant. Miss Turner was ecstatic; if Martina had been her child she couldn't have been happier. To show how proud she was, she gave her three hundred dollars and told her to use it in whatever way she wanted to. Martina had used it to purchase writing books and other school supplies.

Martina was very happy although she had not placed first. She was overjoyed that her friend Leonie was in the same class as she was. They had hugged each other tightly until it hurt when they discovered that they were still together. Terrence had not made it; he was in the second stream. To both Martina and Leonie's great disappointment, Stone Cold had moved up with them. She had regarded them with disdain when she heard their names being called. As usual she installed herself, along with two of her gang members, at the front of the classroom. They tried to engage the attention of all the teachers by answering all the questions asked and volunteering to do all the little chores in the class that the teacher wanted done. When the teachers were absent, they were their true selves, snobbish, bullying and domineering.

Stone Cold had visited Canada over the holidays and she made certain that everyone was aware of this. As soon as the slightest opportunity presented itself, she boasted about all the places she had visited in Ottawa, the capital, and passed around pictures of herself and her family sight seeing, having dinner with family and friends, and shopping. She made certain that Martina and Leonie did not see her pictures. When they had reached the back of the class where the girls were sitting, she decisively monitored them and steered them in another direction. There were questioning looks on the faces of the children who noted this action and a number of them whispered to one another, questioning what she had done.

Martina and Leonie did not appear to be ruffled in any way about Stone Cold's behaviour. They had not expected anything apart from the behaviour exhibited.

They were seated at the back of the class but not beside each other. Leonie was sitting immediately in front of Martina. This was a cosy arrangement for them. They felt like allies fortified to take on academic and Stone Cold darts. Like in grade seven, Martina was installed in an upstairs classroom and commanded the view of two houses with well laid lawns and fruit trees. She sometimes went into the imaginative realm and fancied herself to be an occupant of the houses. She envisioned herself occupying a large bedroom with her own bed and other furniture and wall lined with books: mystery novels, romantic novels, exciting science fiction, adventure stories and educational books. Her imagination reared to further heights and she pictured herself sitting quietly and reading under a grove of trees, or reading by the poolside.

Most exciting of all was the dream of swimming in the pool, moving back and forth in relative peace doing the free style, breast stroke, butterfly stroke and back stroke. She imagined the water, washing her mind free of her domestic problems, soothing her troubled thoughts about violence on the bus and erasing the horrible memory of the burnt body being carried out on the night of the fire. Living in a house like that would certainly cause Stone Cold and her friends to view her from a different angle, not that she really cared about being accepted by them in particular, but to be accepted by others and not to be thought of merely as the girl from the inner city. The voices of the children and teachers, the intrusive bell and the pull of reality would always jolt her back to the present and jeer at her dreams, dreams she would never share with anyone, not even Leonie. One thing was certain though; she was going to make her achievement in swimming a reality, not a dream.

Her grade eight teachers remained the same except for History and Music. She was extremely glad that her Mathematics teacher had remained the same because if she did not have an exceptional Mathematics teacher she would not be able to keep up her standard. For some reason she seemed to have offended the History teacher. She could not really explain why but she seemed to have taken an active dislike for, and to Martina, badgering her for no apparent reason. She never learnt her name or refused to use it as she always referred to her as "You Girl" or "Miss".

It all started in the third week of the term, when she was staring through the window and was walking through her dreams of living in one of the palatial houses. So entrenched was she in this dream that she did not hear the teacher's question which had been directed at her. They were discussing Columbus' voyages and Martina could have easily answered any question based on that topic because she had read the entire chapter in her history book thoroughly. She jumped when the girl beside her intruded in her thoughts by calling her name suddenly, "Martina! Girl you don't hear the teacher asking you a question?"

She stared at her, then at the teacher not knowing what to say.

"You girl stand! What is your name?" the teacher shouted, an angry look on her face.

Martina told her her name and stood up, nervously twirling her pen on the desk.

"Do you have a hearing impairment?" the teacher asked rudely, walking towards her.

Martina interpreted this to mean whether she could hear properly or not and answered, "No Miss I'm alright."

"Well if your hearing is not impaired, then your mind must be. Go and stand at the back at once!"

The class was amused. This diversion from old dead Columbus was very welcomed. They laughed softly, making sounds to show that they were embarrassed for her. The teacher did not comment on the laughter and sounds but continued her lesson.

Leonie felt sad. Couldn't the teacher have repeated the question instead of being so harsh? She knew that her friend knew the answer but somehow had not responded and she wondered why. She knew that Martina was a quiet person and that sometimes she seemed to be thinking of secret things, which she did not talk about. She hardly spoke about her home and when she had tried to glean information about her parents and what they did, Martina had simply said that her mother worked down town and her father was dead. She had told her the first names of her brother and sister and the schools they attended, and stopped there. Leonie noticed that she had her mother's surname though her mother was not married and that she did not mention anything about a stepfather or proffered the surnames of her siblings. She did not talk about her home or community or close relatives as she, Leonie, did. She kept her observation to herself and felt that there was some mystery or something that was not right at home. She had observed her address when she was writing a letter in grade seven and did not question her about it. More than all she pondered about the very light inexpensive lunch that she bought daily, but had dismissed it with the friendly thought that Martina was not a great eater. She had often offered to share her lunch with her, but her kindness was often rebuffed by the explanation that she usually ate a big breakfast.

As she looked at her standing at the back of the class, frail and embarrassed like a sensitive mimosa plant that had been trodden on, her heart drooped within her. She wanted to reach out and hug her as she sometimes did at break, lunchtime or after school. A sudden rush of anger rushed up in defence of her friend. She knew that Stone Cold did not like her mainly because she was poor, but reasoned that her ability and helpfulness was worth more than being able to wear expensive items and visit foreign countries. Martina was always clean and wore her uniform well being naturally blessed with a good bearing even though some good food would have emphasized this more. Her unprocessed hair, one of three in the class, was always neatly combed and her shoes clean, though if one looked carefully polish seemed to be a well desired commodity.

That day marked the beginning of being publicly shouted at or punished for trivialities. A few weeks later their class was engaged in the activity of tracing the world map and highlighting the Caribbean that Columbus had discovered and colonized. Martina was engrossed in her work but was briefly interrupted by Leonie asking her which colour they were to use for each country. Martina started answering her when the teacher's voice attacked her, "You girl sitting on the periphery, whoever asked you to do group work? If I wanted you to work together I would have placed you in groups. Some people obviously do not belong in this class because they obviously cannot work on their own."

All eyes turned to see who was being chided, Martina and Leonie included. Nobody knew what a periphery was and thought it meant something extra placed on a chair, so at first they had no idea who was being addressed and only found out because of the teacher's riveted stare at Martina and Leonie. The girls, feeling the stares of the students on them, dropped their eyes in embarrassment. They did not try to explain because that would have probably made things more difficult.

The teacher walked over to their seat to see what they were doing and Martina felt extremely small in her presence. She made no comments about the girls' work after scrutinizing them, instead she glared at them as a warning and then moved on. The girls were astonished at the teacher's words. They had not been told before that talking was not allowed and moreover they were not actually talking as one could hardly term answering a short question talking. In her mind, many of the parrots in the class who chatted like plugged in engines were never reprimanded, yet they had been embarrassed for asking and answering one little question. She determined at that instance that unless the teacher asked her a question she would not open her mouth except to breathe.

Thus resolved, she started her period of practised silence. This was not difficult for Martina because she was a quiet person. Leonie found this difficult to maintain as she longed to comment when something amusing or interesting was said in history class. Martina knew she would want to do this and purposefully averted her eyes, staring fixedly at the teacher and no one else. This plan of action did not suit the teacher. She made this clear one day when she asked for volunteer answers as to whether Christopher Columbus had actually discovered the Caribbean countries he was said to have discovered. Martina remained silent and still. After a few students had voiced their varying opinions she pounced as if she had been long waiting to spring and the opportune moment had presented itself.

"You girl at the back. Yes, the one to the extreme left. Has your tongue fallen out of your head, or have you swallowed it? You don't participate in this class at all; all you do is sit there."

Martina's reasoning power failed her. How could anyone please a teacher like this? If you talked you were in trouble, if you did not you were still in trouble, all this was too much for her to figure out. She stood up and gave her answer, drawing on information about the previous inhabitants of the islands — and the meaning of the word discovery. Her clear voice, distinct pronunciation and logical reasoning could not be denied. Everyone looked at her; some with admiration and some with envy. She could not tell what the teacher's solid gaze and "Alright that's your opinion" meant. After this Martina kept her silent demeanour, feeling that it was better to be embarrassed for silence than to be garrulous.

Stone Cold enjoyed herself immensely after each encounter, making certain to enact each incident after the teacher's departure. She along with her group of budding dramatists were really having fun mimicking the teacher and imitating Martina's stony stance. She told herself that one day she would avenge her dignity that was being smeared and ridiculed, but not yet. One day, the thought of really having a fist to mouth encounter with the group entered her mind but she thought better of it and continued to ignore Stone Cold and her slightly enlarged group. Miss Turner and her teacher's admonitions kept it in control. Martina decided that the ways of teachers were past finding out and was an undertaking best left for an older, wiser person. She thought that moods and grades were married, but to her surprise, the teacher's insults did not affect her expected grades. This cemented the idea even more that some teachers were strange and unfathomable beings.

CRITICAL

On Milverton's vast compound there were a variety of mangoes. Even before they were fit, they were objects of temptation. Even the most honest person entertained the thought of sinking his or her teeth into the yellow flesh of one of those green and red mangoes, waving temptingly on the branches as if inviting one to pick them. Two grade ten boys, unable to resist the invitation of the colourful mangoes, yielded to temptation and stoned one of the trees that was at the back of the school. It was against the school rules to stone or pick the mangoes but they decided to flaunt this rule.

They had taken a black plastic bag to the scene of the crime and had successfully brought down four of the waving temptations. Looking around and seeing no one, the taller of the two decided to climb the tree. He had learnt how to move as quickly as a wild cat on his holiday visits to the rural area. He ascended the tree and started testing the mangoes to see which ones were ripe or almost ripe. As soon as he wrenched the first one from the branch, a loud voice asked him what he was doing in the tree and commanded him to get down. The boy was so frightened that he dropped the mango on his friend's head. The boy ran off after making a loud howl, leaving his friend to get down out of the tree and make his escape without being caught.

While he was making his escape, the boy in the tree slithered down hastily, ripping his pants at the front of the left side and scraping the exposed area badly. The abrasion did not stop him from running away quickly, leaving the black bag with the mango for the grounds man to pick up. He took them to the principal who asked him to find out the identity of the boys. He had seen both their faces clearly and could identify them as he had seen them hanging around the mango tree. He did not really know their names, but when he described them to a number of boys with whom he was friendly, they supplied the names of the two who thought they had gone undetected.

General worship took place two times, Mondays and Fridays. The principal did not accost them immediately but allowed the boys to think they had gotten away. Apart from worship, announcements were made, promotions done, commendations made and anything else worthy of mention, including misdemeanours, were publicized. The two boys, unaware of the coming public exposure, stood beside each other in worship and participated whole heartedly and even asked for forgiveness of sins (not for climbing the mango tree) when they were told to pray silently.

After the announcements were made and the debating team was called out and congratulated for winning the fourth round and advancing to the quarter finals, the principal took up a purple floral gift bag which had been resting against the podium and pulled out a black transparent bag. The two boys, standing in the middle of the gathering of students, looked at each other in shocked amazement as the principal proceeded to take four mangoes out of the bag. The students started to laugh and some wondered if he was going to sing the folk song, 'Mango Time'.

The principal was a short man and so as not to emphasize his height, he very often moved away from the podium and marched about to and fro as he spoke in his thunderous voice which kind of made his height less conspicuous. The area on which he stood was a raised concrete area which served as a corridor for the administrative block. There were several sets of steps made for accessing this corridor platform, as most people referred to it. The administrative building had a very square, large area of land in front of it which was paved. It was referred to as the quadrangle and was hemmed in by buildings on every side. Worship and most of the stand up functions were held here.

As the children watched, he picked up two of the mangoes, one in each hand, and bellowed for Troy Albert and Zane

McDowell to report to the platform. They made their way slowly with heads bowed. As soon as they got there, the principal began his speech.

"Ladies and gentlemen, I want you to treat what I am going to say with the utmost solemnity. There is to be no snickering or talking while I am speaking. Two days ago, two of your schoolmates decided to join the criminal elements in this society."

He paused for awhile and looked around at the children's faces hoping to see some trace of alarm and condemnation, but there was none whatever. What he saw was restrained amusement threatening to erupt into outbursts of laughter at anytime. He walked to one end of the platform and then back to the middle, held up the two mangoes and continued.

"Ladies and gentlemen, I ask, where does criminal activity begin? Is it with the knife? Is it with the gun or any other weapon? I tell you no. Sometimes it begins with very minute things, a sweet, a spoon of sugar, a little milk poured into the palm and yes, stolen mangoes! Stolen mangoes, taken without permission from the trees on the school property."

He paused again and paced the platform with a sombre look on his face. Somewhere in the crowd a student tittered, unable to hold back the pressing laughter. The principal looked around suddenly, hoping to detect the offender and bring him or her to justice but all he saw were faces filled with repressed laughter. Appearing to gain more strength from the pause, he continued to speak and moved towards the edge of the platform.

"Too many times offenders are not punished for the offence committed, but here at Milverton, that will not happen. These two juvenile law breakers will be punished severely! Oh yes they will be!" His voice became extremely irate and he started stuttering. "Th-the-they will be pun...!"

His words trailed off in the air and all the subdued laughter broke free and chimed out loudly, because the principal, in his anger, had gone too closely to the edge of the platform and had fallen right over the edge still clutching the two mangoes in his hands! Two students who were standing in front of him were the unwilling recipients of the sudden weight which bore down on them, bringing them swiftly to the ground.

One of the vice principals, Mr. Brompton, and a number of teachers who were standing close to the front, rushed forward and assisted both the fallen principal who was still clutching the mangoes, and the two students who were crying more from shock than from pain. Chaos was given free rein. The students pressed forward whooping and hitting one another's back, unable to stand straight or speak coherently. They pushed one another and stepped on feet that were in the way, all in a bid to make it to the front to get first hand view of the bewildered and hurting principal.

The second vice principal, Mrs. Dawes, ran to the platform, took up the microphone and appealed for quiet and sanity, but no one heeded her plea and soon she put down the mike and retired to the side where the other teachers were standing. For the next twenty minutes, even after the principal had been taken away, held on both sides by the vice principal and the

Religious Education teacher, the laughter and unruliness persisted. One girl started vomiting and the students drew back suddenly as if they had been hit, leaving her to cover her mouth and run to the bathroom. One boy wet his pants and had to spend most of the day in the bathroom with his shirt out, covering his pants.

After approximately half an hour, the teachers finally gained some semblance of order and ushered the children to their classrooms, while they attended an emergency staff meeting. The ridicule and disorder continued as the students satirized the headmaster. In almost every classroom there were dramatists on stage re-enacting the principal's 'mango dive', as the incident was later named.

Martina sat in her seat trying her best to keep the laughter and the hunger pain from consuming her. She had enjoyed herself thoroughly just like any other student. Tears had coursed in spate, without permission, down her face. She was not really laughing at the principal, as many students stoutly declared later on, but the manner in which he had fallen. An ordinary person falling in a less dramatic way was always an object of comedy not to mention someone of high social standing as a principal. This was inconceivable and Martina spared no sympathy as she laughed. Seeing the principal limping as he was being helped to his office had sobered her for a little while, but when she remembered the amusing fall, the tears started again. Not even the hunger tugging at her stomach was able to detract from the amusement.

Leonie was absent. She had waited for her at the gate that morning but when her mother came only her brother came out of the car. She always felt lonely when Leonie was absent. She would be quite vexed when she heard about the mango dive and expressed her unluckiness at having missed the event of the year.

She was also sad that Leonie was absent because on that particular day she would not have refused to partake of her lunch if she had offered. For some reason that week was an even more financially embarrassing week than any other in her home. Her mother had told her at the beginning of the week that she could only attend school for three days because she had to use some of her lunch money to add to the little she had to pay for a visit to the doctor.

Martina thought that her mother looked physically deflated since her fight with Shimron. She still went out at odd times but maybe one less time per week. Even though Martina felt sorry for her, she thought it was unfair that it was her attendance to school that had to suffer. She definitely did not want to stop from school. That would certainly hamper her work as many of the children at her school were selfish and did not like to share notes or give homework to absentees. Only one's close friend could be depended on to extend that service. That practice had caused students' averages to fall, because if you missed a piece of work, unless you could prove that you were ill or had other extenuating circumstances, your marks would be divided all the same by the number of pieces of work given. She wanted no low average or second hand information. She wanted to be at school to hear for herself. As a result, she decided that she would save some of her money for the five days bus fare and eat lunch only two days.

She ate lunch on Monday and Wednesday, and had a meagre snack on Thursday, so on Friday she was extremely hungry. It didn't help the situation when she ate only once in the afternoon after going home on Thursday and had only a slice of bread with a cup of mint tea earlier that morning. When the principal had displayed the mangoes, she had secretly wished that she could get even one of them to eat at lunch time, she was so hungry. The hunger was seeping through her body and affecting both the physical and mental faculties. Her head felt a little unsettled as if the heavy substances which comprised her brain had somehow become watery and were slightly moving around.

She was very glad that the teachers were not in the classrooms because concentration on the academics would prove to be too arduous. Writing would also be difficult because her hands, of their own accord, felt slightly tremulous as if they were being moved by an invisible wind or tremor. In addition to that, there was a prickly pain in the chest region. It was as if somehow a pointed object had found its way into her stomach. Not standing up well to the painful assault, her stomach groaned in protest at each prick.

Martina rested her hands on the desk and put her head on her hands. She earnestly prayed to fall asleep, but somehow felt that if she fell asleep she would not be able to wake up. Her mouth had become very dry and she folded her lips, moistening them with her tongue. Her feet, responding to the pain from the rest of her body, felt as if all substances had drained from them and were no longer solid states of matter but had changed to liquid. She was thankful that she could sit undisturbed, because if a teacher should walk into the classroom she would stand as the rule dictated and at that very moment standing was something her body seemed to have suspended until it got the replenishment it needed.

Miraculously, she fell asleep and slept for almost an hour. How she was able to do that in all the noise must have been attained from her years of sleeping through the loud weekend music in the lane. A student was passing her desk and accidentally bounced against it. The desk shifted and Martina was shaken out of her sleep. For awhile she was disoriented and seemed to have lost her sense of reality. She stared around foolishly for awhile and then unreality gave way to reality and she started to focus and realized that she was in her classroom at school; the clock on the wall told her that it would soon be lunchtime and she wondered what she would do then.

There was a pressing need for her to go to the bathroom and she decided to comply. She got up unsteadily, her feet having gained strength during her sleep. She made her way slowly pass two other grade eight classrooms and barely had the strength to wave to Terrence who shouted to her when she was passing his classroom. She was glad that he did not run out to talk to her as he usually did because she had to keep moving or her feet, that were losing their strength again, would surrender and then she would be the centre of the second comedy act for the day. On her way from the bathroom she had to pass the administrative block. This was normally a quiet area and students were constantly reminded not to make the area a public thoroughfare and should be seen there only if they had business to conduct or were on their way to assembly. Martina did not see anyone in the area so she cut across the quadrangle in order to save the time and strength instead of going all the way around the building and then up the stairs.

As she was going across the quadrangle, she noticed two mangoes lying on the ground. They were the same mangoes that had disgraced the two boys and the principal. Going up close to them she realized that even though they seemed a bit bruised, having gone through the traumatic experience of first being stoned, and then trodden on in that fateful morning incident, they were not unfit and could be eaten. Without even thinking, she picked up the mango closest to her and pushed it into her uniform pocket. Ignoring the pains piercing her stomach, she walked briskly to the back of the school. There was a pipe close to the ancillary workers' station, none of them was in so she hastily washed the mango and retreated to a tree nearby where she hid and bit into the mango as if it was the most succulent thing she had ever tasted. After washing her mouth she took the same short cut she had taken earlier on through the quadrangle. This time the area was not empty, Virgil was there and he was bending down and picking up the second mango that she had left behind.

School was dismissed earlier than usual that day. It seemed as if the teachers had only just started teaching in the afternoon when the bell rang. As soon as the last metallic peal had faded away, an announcement was made which summoned the whole student body to the quadrangle, which seemed to have become the most popular place in the school. Every single teacher present at school was there. They all stood with their classes and had the class registers in their hands. They marked the names of the students, taking time to ascertain those who were said to be really absent and not being truant. Martina noted that the names were called at least three times and empathic questions asked about the absentees. She had a disquieting feeling that something unpleasant was in the fore because only in cases of emergency or a fire or earthquake drill were they shepherded to the quadrangle at this time and the register marked. The registers were always marked after the second bell each morning and right after lunchtime.

After making certain that the registration activity was through, Mr. Brompton went to the platform. It was observed that he did not stand near to the edge of the platform, neither did he pace. All eyes were riveted at him, but he stood there for a time not saying anything as if he was punishing the students by making them stand there doing nothing. The students sensed his mood and not wanting to annoy him, they remained quiet. He stood there for more than a minute, arms folded, surveying the students and teachers. It was as if the principal had died and he had asked for a minute of silence and was waiting for everyone to finish observing this. Martina would not have been surprised if the vice principal had said, "May his soul rest in peace and life perpetual shine on him."

There was a slight movement towards the seniors' section of the gathering and everyone turned to see the boy who had been injured in the school feud on the bus, speak to a nearby teacher and then hobbled to one of the stone benches at the far end of the quadrangle and sat. Everyone watched him closely as if he had done something important and then turned again to Mr. Brompton whose eyes had also followed the boy to the stone bench. Deciding that he had kept them in suspense long enough, he ran his hand across his forehead and started speaking. One could not escape the look of triumph on his face.

"Ladies and gentlemen," he began in a tone that was clearly mocking and seemed to be saying 'Ladies and gentlemen indeed', "this morning you displayed the most disgraceful behaviour anyone has ever seen in the history of this excellent institution."

He paused, allowing the words to bury themselves in what he hoped was the repentant minds of the students. He continued, "You will never and I underline never, be allowed to get away with this low, sick behaviour! Your behaviour reflects the disgraceful society from which you come. We are trying to purge you of this disgrace but the demented society is still in you. We are trying to stop the cords of evil from binding you but you have become so entangled in them that we cannot identify you differently from the cord. Well, as one of the laws of science testifies, for every action there is an equal and opposite reaction. My fine ladies and gentlemen your punishment is as follows..."

He paused and surveyed the gathering, a spark of amusement dancing in his eyes. He seemed to be enjoying a secret joke the students could not guess at.

"You," he continued, "will report for school tomorrow."

"Sir, tomorrow is Saturday," one student shouted, amazed at the idea that the teacher was forgetting that school was not held on a Saturday.

"You are indeed a brilliant student. I award you full marks for your knowledge!" He smiled at the boy. "Tomorrow is Saturday indeed, and tomorrow you will all report for school at seven thirty sharp in your uniforms!"

A loud buzz of anger and shocked disbelief filled the air all around. The students looked at one another mystified, mortified, and incredulous. They had never heard anything of the kind, school on a Saturday! They would certainly be comic relief for everyone. They would never be able to let this one die! They would become mockery material for all the other high schools.

The vice principal, pretending there had been no show of anger continued, "The grounds men have been instructed not to clean up the compound for the day as you will do this quite efficiently tomorrow. When you get here you will also be instructed about your other duties. Before I forget, I must warn you there should be no sneakers or white socks and everyone must have his or her school bag or folder. Anyone who is present today and absent tomorrow will be absent for three days and a report on their insubordination will be written and placed on each file. You may turn around and lead off in your lines. Enjoy your day tomorrow."

Martina walked towards the school gate. Everyone was talking and quarrelling in groups. She found herself walking in a group with Hairnet Deacon and three other students from her class. She abandoned her usual quiet disposition and spoke as angrily as the next student. She pointed out that it was unfair for only the students to be punished as some of the teachers were also laughing when the principal had done the mango dive. She supplied names such as Miss Henry, the science teacher; Mrs. Gayle, the Physical Education teacher; and Mrs. Beeves had laughed so much that she had covered her mouth and then moved to stand behind the Mathematics teacher. She wondered aloud at the absence of the staff's sense of humour, but Hairnet pointed out that if they had just laughed and stopped it wouldn't have been that bad, but they had gone on and on for minutes even after they were told to stop. He defiantly swore that he would prefer to be suspended rather than leaving his home on any Saturday to clean up a dirty old school! One girl in the group said that her parents would give her additional punishment when they heard about the incident. She bemoaned the fact that she would have to spend her recreational time doing chores as she would have to spend the whole day at school doing other people's job all because the principal had behaved as if stoning mangoes was not an ordinary normal part of boyhood but a criminal offence. Martina knew her mother would say, "When pickney can't hear dem mus' feel." She proved to be quite right about that.

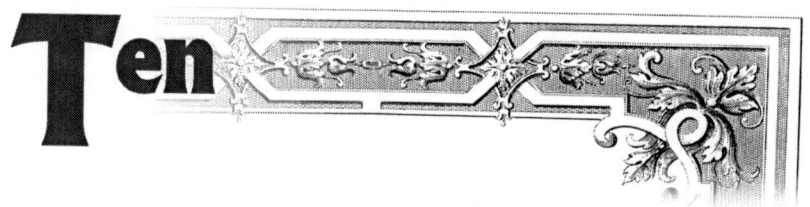

Ten

Shimron got off the bus three stops before he got to school. He stood for a while watching the bus drive away. After it was out of sight he remained standing in the same position watching other buses come and go. He soon got tired of standing and sat on one of the crossbars at the bus stop. He sat with ease as if this was a position he was accustomed to sitting in frequently. From where he sat, he could see much of the town and its activity quite clearly. On both sides of the street and all around the round-about there were business places. Most of them were single storey buildings and a few were two storey buildings. The buildings were in varying degrees of physical condition. Some of them appeared to have been around since the eighteenth century as was evidenced by their particular architecture of brown bricks. Looking at them, one got a sense of history or a strong presence of the past. Alongside them were more modern buildings brightly painted with large shutters and double doors. A few of the buildings were crying out for their paintwork to be revisited.

Though it was early morning, there was much activity on the street. Store clerks and other workers hurried into buildings or past buildings seeming anxious to be punctual for work. A few of them stopped to converse briefly and then moved on. The vendors were out early with their large transparent bags of drink and snack items. They were advertising their products, lauding and inviting potential customers to view what they had. There were some who even tried to undersell others by lowering their prices and discrediting the other vendors. There were the street vendors who plied their products by moving around tirelessly. The higher calibres of vendors also solicited customers but on a more sophisticated level. They did not walk around but sat cross-legged or leant in front of their stalls located behind the stores. They were known as ICIs, Informal Commercial Importers, who had acquired enough finances to travel abroad and shop, and then return to Jamaica to sell their goods at sometimes exorbitant prices. The justifications for the prices were expensive plane fares, hotel rates, goods and customs fees. Some of them had succeeded financially and had bought expensive vehicles and built large houses in the suburbs and prestigious hilly areas in the city. Many people surmised that involvement in drugs was also a factor in their swift affluence.

Shimron's ambition was to be like one of these upscale vendors. He liked the large gold chains reaching all the way to one's waist or navel and the expensive name brand jerseys, jeans and sneakers they wore. The wrist, burdened by large costly watches and bright gold rings "bawling out" from as many as six or eight fingers greatly drew his attention. That was the life he wanted. He did not want to work for anyone in the world. He wanted to be master of his own business going and coming as he pleased without anyone ordering him around or treating him like a child. He wanted freedom to live as he wanted to. School for him was good until you could read and write properly and then it lost its appeal and became a prison where the teachers tried to fill ones head with boring, unreal and unnecessary ideas which were for people who wanted to waste their lives trying to make sense of what life was all about.

He didn't need any school to tell him what life was all about as he had learnt that from very early in his life. It was about hunger, being deprived of the ordinary things in life that made you feel like a human being. It was about not living in a good house with a good bathroom and having to wait for more than an hour to use something that was supposed to represent one. It was about sharing the same little box room with two girls and sleeping on an ancient mattress with wires and other itchy things poking into you whenever you moved or whatever position you slept in. It was about getting a meagre sum for bus fare and lunch with the great expectation that you would become a Rhodes Scholar or end up in one of the high class professions. It was about not being able to wear any really good clothes and wishing with all your heart that somehow you could get some somewhere. It was always having to eat tin food and vegetables most of the time and wishing that the smell of good meals being cooked could be coming from your kitchen instead of the neighbours' or good restaurants. It was no father to care for you or play games with you like the model families on the television or in picture books. It was hell, pure wretched hell!

He thought that poor people like Martina who had a brain could go on deluding themselves that education was going to help them squash their poverty. He knew that even if you passed a few subjects or learnt a skill, the minute you wrote your address on an application form your chances would evaporate. People living below a certain area in the city were supposed to be thieves, rapists and gunmen so who would want to have them in their businesses? The girls ended up pregnant from an early age, sometimes bearing children for different men, each time seeking a better standard of living.

Well, he was not bright, that was Martina's forte. She could go on attending her posh school. He wondered where she got the ability from. It must be from the father that she didn't have. That made them equal, no father, both of them must be some strange creatures that had just materialized out of nothingness and had attached themselves to the first human being they had encountered, their mother. Well his mother could always waste her time talking because he was finished with school and one day soon he would be finished with her as well! It was more exciting to have fun and earn a little cash each day and that was what he was going to do!

Having further cemented his resolve, he jumped from the iron bar, dodged in and out of slow moving vehicles and made his way down a street which was behind one of the old stores. The street was very narrow with large potholes that were comfortably at home because they had been a part of the street for years. A number of them had large tufts of grass growing in them. During the rainy season, water collected in the holes and provided a playground for mosquitoes. The houses on either side of the street were in a dilapidated condition. The ones made from concrete were crying out for urgent attention as there were huge zigzag cracks running from one beam to the foundation. Many doors, battered by the elements, had rough pieces of wood nailed across them. There was more than a hint that it had been a long time ago since these houses had had a pleasant encounter with paint. The wooden ones were even worse. The exterior of many had dried dirt and other unknown substances clinging to them, some of them leaned drunkenly to one side and seemed ready to collapse if the elements became a little rough. The houses were protected by zinc and hard cardboard fences, some of them leaning forward because a proper foundation was missing.

Shimron marched through the community as if he lived there. He passed mothers accompanying their young children to the bus stop; older children, unaccompanied, going to the bus stop; people catching water at a standpipe; people going to work; small groups of young men arguing and mothers shouting to children or gossiping at the edge of the community. He pushed a zinc gate, went inside and sat on a piece of broken block. He took a tee-shirt from his bag and quickly changed into it then loosely folded his khaki shirt and placed it inside his school bag. It appeared as if he was waiting for someone. While he waited he took out a knife and examined it closely. It was not very long and had a brown handle and a straight blade. He tested its sharpness by cutting blades of grass growing nearby. He had owned the knife for about three years now and never went anywhere without it.

After approximately fifteen minutes, another school boy pushed the gate and joined Shimron, then another came and over the next fifteen minutes eight of them had gathered. Among them were also three men ages twenty to thirty-five from the community. They set up some sound boxes and started playing music. Shimron and the others danced to the music, gyrating and contorting their bodies, slapping one another's back when an excellent move was made and punctuating their dancing and noise with expletives.

With the music pounding in the background, they turned their attention to some rough pieces of board placed on several blocks and large hunks of wood. These were used as tables for gambling which they would spend most of their time doing. Each table had one of the three men from the community in charge. They played different card games such as "blackjack", "three a card" and "strip me".

They gambled for hours, stopping only to tend the food that was being cooked on a two burner kerosene oil stove and to seek the attention of young girls who passed by frequently. The girls stopped only for the men from the community, only waving to or completely ignoring the other boys. After lunch they lit up ganja pipes and joints, inhaling and puffing out in an exaggerated manner. Shimron floated to an unknown place where all was peaceful and happy. There were no problems or intruding adults, only happiness and heaven. He floated off right onto one of the makeshift tables. He awoke sometime later to the sound of earthly reggae music instead of the one he had heard during his hallucinations. He shook his head vigorously to bring himself back to reality and continued lying for a while, wondering why his sojourn in the peaceful world had to be so brief. Why couldn't he stay there forever and be free?

He decided that he didn't want to gamble any more that day. A streak of luck had visited him and he had no intention of losing it. The community men always encouraged them to continue gambling after they had won a considerable amount but this was so they could win back the money for themselves. Shimron had other plans for the money and didn't want to lose it so he laid there and pretended to be asleep. He heard the others joking about the effect of the weed on him, "Bwoy, Shimron caa handle the weed. Him might end up walking the streets like dat yute dat use to hang with we," said one of the men, almost falling to the ground from laughing so hard.

"No man, mi no t'ink so, it jus' mek him sleep. Mi no see him do nutten crazy or talk stupid when him smoke it," replied another.

Shimron listened to them and smiled inwardly. They thought he was going to end up mad, well he wouldn't! His future plans did not include being an inmate of any insane asylum. He wanted to have money so that he could help his family even though he was not certain they liked him anymore. Since the fight on the night of the fire, his mother had left him alone. She did not speak to him and only acknowledged his presence by furtively looking at him whenever they happened to cross paths in the house. He noticed that she did not seem to be her usual self. She seemed to have crept inside herself and remained there. This behaviour was not only directed at him but at his sisters. She spoke to them, but not as effusively as she used to. She even seemed a little frail.

He had noticed, on one of his rare early visits at home that Martina was regarding her a little sadly, looking at her, then at him. He felt that she was blaming him for her withdrawal. If the truth was to be exposed, it would be surprising to learn that he did feel sorry about fighting with her. He had not planned it, it had just happened because she had kept badgering him about stupid old school, coming home early and all the things that mothers felt was their God given right to preach at children about. He knew that the other boys defied and disobeyed their mothers, but none of them had mentioned fighting with them. He did not tell any of his friends about the fight, because even though he had become angry and pained inside, he knew it was wrong to fight with one's mother. As soon as he could get enough money, he would leave and live on his own. He did not want to see her every time and be reminded of his evil deed.

He didn't like Martina thinking badly of him either, out of the two sisters, he preferred her to Yvette. Loud Yvette definitely needed some of the quiet ways of her sister who sometimes did not seem to be like the rest of the family. There was an undefined quality about her that made her seem to belong at a better place with a different family. He again wondered who her father was and why their mother never mentioned him even if it was just to tell the girl his name and where he was from. He sometimes wished he could find out and tell her.

On a few occasions he had noticed some of the boys in the lane watching her lasciviously as she passed them. She was now in grade nine and he knew that a number of girls in the lane had become pregnant at her age. He wished that she would focus on her lessons, even though he didn't know where this would take her in life. Lessons did not seem to work for them in the lane as it did for people who already had money. He wished he could find a way to encourage her not to get involved with boys and end up just like their mother. He wished he could protect her. He knew so many of the dangers that were out there waiting for young girls like her; the womanizers who thought they had the right to any girl they wanted.

He remembered the fight on the bus which had ended at the bus terminus on the street the day when Martina had gone to school on a Saturday dressed up in school uniform. A group of boys from two other schools had mercilessly teased the boys from Milverton High and a fight had ensued again on the bus and ended up with two of them being stabbed with knives. Luckily no one had died due to the intervention of the people standing at the bus stop and the quick action of the police.

He fell asleep again and when he woke up he collected his things and made ready to go. Everyone was getting ready to go. As he was going through the gate, one of the community men beckoned to him and asked him to remain behind. He was very uncomfortable about this because he knew that these men, even though they acted friendly towards them, were not to be trusted. The man took his time to put away the pots and pieces of boards and then he came purposefully towards the slightly apprehensive Shimron. Looking him straight in the face he asked directly, "Can you get out of your house at night?"

Shimron thought that this was an odd question and wondered what he was up to, but he still answered in the affirmative.

The next question took him by surprise. "How would you like to make a little easy money?" The man had a sneaky smile on his face as if he already anticipated what the answer would be.

Shimron was generally surprised at the question. He certainly would like to make some extra money as long as he didn't have to hurt or kill anyone. "Yes, I could use some," he answered anxiously, yet a little nervously.

"Good, it easy like drinking wata. All you have to do is get to the stone statue by the corner of North Parade and wait behind it. Somebody will come to you and ask you the name of the street where you gamble. Just answer the question and he will give you a bag and tell you where to take it. Don't ask no question; jus' take the bag an' move fast. When you come in the morning, a will give you a envelope, cool?"

It sounded very cool indeed. Cool, easy and quick. Shimron could not believe it! Here was his chance to make some money. He would wait until after his first delivery, see how it paid and then he would take it from there. As he walked towards the bus stop he was already planning how much to spend and how much to save. He would stop pretending to go to school and announce generally that he had a job downtown. He reasoned that he would not be telling a lie because the delivery was a job, wasn't it? Well, not the ordinary nine to five job, but he would leave home as usual and continue the gambling. Shimron was so taken up with the idea of making quick, easy money that he did not consider the dangers, what he would be delivering and to whom. All he thought about was the money and an explanation as to how he had acquired it.

That afternoon he got home at about five thirty. It was his intention to get a good sleep, have a good meal at a restaurant, compliments of his gambling proceeds, watch a movie and then keep his appointment.

Martina was shocked to see Shimron at home that early. She was even more surprised that he greeted her so warmly and seemed in the mood for a little conversation. He enquired about school and the situation on the bus. He even asked her if she had heard that Julie was walking up and down the road talking foolishness and shouting to her children to get out of the house before the fire burns them to death. Martina, glad at the change in him, spoke freely to him, wishing that their mother was there and could join in the conversation. Shimron took the opportunity to tell Martina that he might be getting a little job downtown soon. Her protestations that he should finish school were met by firm determination that school was not for him and that he would be better off working and trying to help himself. Nothing she could say shook his decision.

After sleeping, he got up, managed to get into the bathroom without joining a line, got ready and bolted outside, completely ignoring Martina's enquiry as to where he was going. He wanted to get to his destination before the time, but wisdom told him that he should not go to the designated spot and wait around too long as passers-by might become suspicious. He took his time eating and watched the movie half way through, and then he hurriedly left and caught a bus just as he got to the bus stop. When he got off the bus, he lingered at the stop for another fifteen minutes and then he walked towards the arranged area. He hid in the shadow of some stone columns and then he went and stood by the statue.

When the time came, nobody appeared except a few people who were going about their business. He went back among the shadows cast by the columns for a while, waiting and watching anxiously. He soon noticed a man who had come suddenly out of the shadows close to him. He was wearing dark clothing and had a cap pulled down over his face so Shimron saw nothing of his face. Shimron walked over to the statue and stood on the side less exposed to the road. The man approached him and asked the prearranged question. Shimron answered as he had been instructed and the man handed him a shopping bag and told him where to leave it. He then left without saying another word.

Shimron walked back into the shadows and then quickly walked three blocks down the road without looking behind him. He thought that if he behaved like a normal pedestrian no one would pay undue attention to him. He reached the designated area and placed the bag where he was instructed. When he had gone a little distance away, he glanced back and was just in time to see a dark shadow disappearing around the corner.

Shimron got up earlier than usual the next morning and went to his gambling area long before anyone else got there. The first one to get there after him was the community man who had recruited him for the nocturnal rendezvous. He handed him a small brown envelope and then left. Shimron went into the old house and smiled as he opened the envelope.

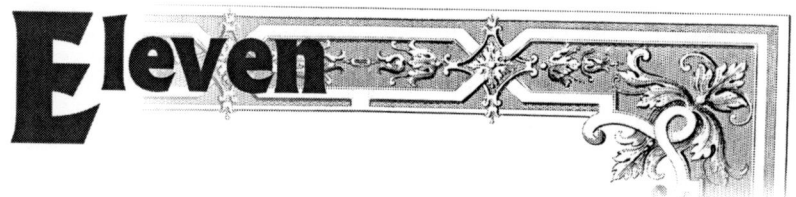

Eleven

9m's form teacher entered the classroom and all the children stood and chorused, "Good morning Mrs. Lyn".

"Good morning class," she answered, but they could all see that from her response it was morning indeed, but the good part of it was questionable.

She did not tell them to sit, but stood surveying them one by one as if they had committed an unpardonable offence. When she got tired of standing and scrutinizing them, she sat with her face in her hand and looked straight ahead of her without focusing on anyone in particular. She pulled back the chair noisily and started pacing with her arms folded. She started looking at them closely again and when her gaze seemed to lock on Martina, she shuddered slightly without knowing why.

She shifted her gaze from the teacher's and started pushing the pen top in and out. She had no idea why the teacher had them standing for so long and was staring at them in such an accusatory manner. To speak for herself, she was not aware of having committed any misdemeanour and she resented being punished along with the rest of the class when she had done nothing to deserve it. She started searching her mind for anything that could have incurred her annoyance. She was always such a friendly teacher, with an aura that invited one to feel comfortable and relaxed in her presence. Her form time activities were always interesting and instead of hating form time as she usually did in grade eight, she looked forward to it in grade nine. It was their form time at that period, but instead of another exciting activity, they were all imitating soldiers on the parade, but did not know the appropriate movements and so remained still.

As if she had run out of the ability to stare any longer, she commanded them to sit without making any unnecessary sounds or else they would all kneel this time. When they were all seated, she began speaking solemnly.

"It has been brought to my attention that a number of students in this class have been losing valuable property since the beginning of the Easter Term."

She paused for a moment, looked around at everyone again and then continued.

"Shauna-Gaye has lost her cellular phone; Tricia-Anne, her calculator; John-Ray, his very expensive Rolex watch which was snatched from his school bag during Physical Education; Camika, her mother's three thousand dollars that was supposed to have paid her parents' telephone bill; and yesterday, Helenetta, her cellular phone."

As she read the items and the owners, she paused at each one and looked at everyone as if she somehow hoped to get a confession. Getting none, she continued,

"This is even more serious than you can possibly think because it means we have a professional thief in our midst.

Not for one moment do I think that the thief is from another class. The person who is doing all of this knows where each student will be at specific times and also where their valuables are kept." She continued by pointing out the graveness of the situation and warned the offender that if he or she was caught, expulsion would be instant.

While she was speaking, the guidance counsellor came in and as soon as the form teacher had finished her speech, she continued with chapter two which was basically a repetition of what had gone on before except that she encouraged the guilty student to reveal his or herself to her, promising not to reveal the identity as she only wanted to save the person from a horrible end by helping to steer him or her on the narrow road to honesty.

Martina listened to both of them, wondering if the offender would really want to turn his or herself in. She couldn't help wondering who was responsible and why the person had stolen all those items. She thought that even though she was the poorest child in the class and probably the whole school, she would never steal from students. Sometimes she had been terribly hungry and still she had not stolen, and if she had to, it would only be to stem her hunger. She wondered how the person had been able to avoid detection so many times, as most of the times except for lunch time, Physical Education, Home Economics and the Sciences, there were always students in the classroom. She wondered if the person was playing a prank or was a serious thief.

That day when she went to swimming, she really gave it her all. The water did not fail to perform its usual soothing magic. It washed away all the thoughts of class problems and all the problems she had at home. She forgot about Stone Cold, Shimron's irregular coming and going, her mother's increasingly tired looks and the money that she needed for the new recommended text for Mathematics. The Mathematics book had not been placed on the book list at the beginning of the school year, but the Mathematics teacher had recommended it a month later. Martina did not even bother to ask her mother to buy it because she knew she had no money. Instead, she was forced to share with Leonie and spent much of her lunch time and a little time before going to swimming copying the homework from Leonie's book. She felt embarrassed because she was the only one in her class who did not have the book. But that day, as she swam, she forgot her embarrassment and put everything into her swimming. At the end of practice, the teacher called everyone together.

She was very nervous and her heart picked up the signal and started drumming irregularly and loudly as if it wanted everyone within earshot to know her emotional state. She was nervous because that afternoon she would find out if she had been elected as a member of the school team. She told them they were all good swimmers but some were exceptional. She warned those who would hear their names after she had finished speaking that if they became complacent, they would be replaced by others. She also cautioned them that being on the team meant even more dedication and harder work. She opened a file jacket she was holding in her hand and started to read the names.

Martina listened anxiously, expectantly hoping and at the same time chiding herself for hoping. After the fifth name had been called, she told herself that she would definitely have to work harder next time around if she wanted to be included. She was so busy admonishing herself that when she heard her name, she shouted out "present miss" instead of making an exultant sound like the others had. Everyone laughed. She could not believe it even though she had dreamt of it so often. A warm feeling of happiness rushed through her body like fire that had been ignited by too much fuel. The tears pulled at her eyelids trying to free themselves, but she pulled them back forcefully, forbidding them to betray her happiness. At last she had a feeling that she was a part of the school, the warm glow of a sense of belonging covered her. She didn't care whether she became popular, as all those who shone at sports normally were, her happiness hinged on being able to achieve something that was very important to her and being called upon to represent her school. She did not love too much attention, did not know how to react to it and when she was happy about something, she always became quiet and wondered how long it would last.

She reminisced about the year she had passed her GSAT for this exclusive school, everyone at her old school seemed to have something to say to her and when she got tired of saying thank you or smiling shyly, she took refuge in her books. She had no books to take refuge in now and only the team members and a few of the aspiring members shook her hand and congratulated her, so she shook hands and smiled back softly.

The heartiest congratulations were given by Tian, who was a member of the boy's swimming team. He lingered over his congratulations and engaged Martina in a brief conversation about swimming competitions and places that they would visit to improve her swimming techniques and keep her place on the team. As he was speaking to a very receptive Martina, a grade eleven girl came up and interrupted the conversation. She ignored Martina and spoke directly to Tian.

"Tian, you better come now or else you will have to walk home!"

She turned her back to Martina as she spoke. Tian ignored her urgent words and introduced her to Martina instead. When the girl turned reluctantly to face her, Martina stared at her as if there was something strange or alarming about her. The physical features that stared back at her were very much like hers. The eyes, the nose and the shape of her face were similar to Martina's. The basic differences were the length of the hair and the girl's fair complexion. She stared back at Martina without interest or even the slightest indication that she had observed anything unusual. It was Tian who commented on the likeness. "I knew when I first saw you Martina that you looked like somebody I know, but it's just now that I am seeing you two together that I am just realizing who you really look like."

He looked from one to the other and then said, "It is a very popular belief that everyone has someone that he or she resembles and you two certainly look alike!"

Neither of the two girls commented and Martina could sense that the other girl did not like the idea at all. She looked condescendingly at Martina, and then back at Tian. "Come man, hurry!"

Tian walked off leaving Martina to ponder about what had just happened. It was the first time that she was seeing that girl even though she had been at the school for almost three years. Tian was not the first person to have made the comment about her resembling somebody at the school. In the eighth grade a teacher had asked her if she knew Sanjay Patterson, an eleventh grader, and she had told her no. She realized that this must be the girl, unless there were three people who looked alike at the same school. Well, she wouldn't make it bother her. The girl was much taller and bigger than she was, so not many people would mistake one for the other. She changed and collected her belongings and went home, forgetting the girl and everyone else, and exulted in the joyful feeling of being an important part of an excellent school.

When she got home, she saw Miss Turner hanging out clothes at the front yard. Not being able to contain herself, she rushed up to her and after greeting her, gushed out the news. Miss Turner dropped the clothes pins and clothes she was holding in her hand into the wash basin and hugged Martina. As she congratulated her, you could hear the tears in her voice. She always hailed Martina's achievements as if they were hers or her offspring's. That afternoon was one of the rare occasions when Martina's mother was at home. She was lying in her bed watching television. Yvette, now in grade seven, was in the children's room doing her home work. As soon as she greeted them both, she threw down her schoolbag and out rushed the great news. Her mother and sister were elated. Yvette slapped her playfully on the back several times shouting out, "Wicked my girl!" while her mother got out of bed, hugged her and smiled at her; a real smile which involved her whole face and eyes, a smile that stayed on her face the whole evening. She did not go out that night, but that did not stop Yvette from slipping out the back door and telling her friends and all who were close by about Martina's good fortune. When Shimron came home for a little while that night, Martina did not even get a chance to tell him of her achievement as Yvette met him at the door with the news.

At school the next day, Martina could not help seeing the envious and curious looks of some of the students who pointed her out or turned to stare at her. In her class, a number of students tried to engage her in an argument about swimming. Martina answered politely as she realized that some of them were only trying to be friends because they thought that she was going to be popular. Stone Cold was clearly not moving with the popularity crowd. She and her friends kept their distance.

After the first two sessions, when the teacher had left the class for some unaccountable reason, Martina felt a tremor sweep over her. She looked up and saw Stone Cold regarding her with an amused look as if she was enjoying a secret joke which involved Martina. Martina would have preferred to see an unfriendly glare as she was accustomed to. The amused look did not quite fit and it caused Martina to wonder what Stone Cold was up to. Maybe she was inventing a story to spread among the student population to discredit her honest selection in the swimming team. Martina felt cold and uncomfortable even though the weather was very warm and she had been sweating a few minutes earlier. She gave Stone Cold a contrasting hostile stare and then turned to speak to Leonie.

The following day after a very frugal lunch, Martina walked back to her classroom with Leonie. Leonie was chattering away furiously about a grade ten boy who was showing too much interest in her, but Martina's mind had swerved into another direction and she was not listening to Leonie anymore as thoughts of her mother and brother occupied her mind. Her mother was going out a little less these days and when she stayed home she spent most of her time in bed. When the girls inquired about her health they were told that she had picked up a virus and would soon feel better. Martina thought that the virus must be a very persistent, malicious one because it had had a tenacious grip on her mother for some months now. She visited the doctor more often now and did very little work around the house. She still went to her week-end job and still received the few dollars from Yvette's father, but financially she seemed worse off. Martina did not get lunch money everyday and was hungry more often than not. It was Shimron who voluntarily gave her money sometimes when he was at home and realized she would have to stay away from school.

Now he was another cause of her worries. He left early in the morning and came home very late at night. He claimed to be working downtown but there was very little evidence of a salary. Yes, he had bought some new clothes, but did not offer to help out financially in the house. Their mother had to pay all the bills and buy the little food they existed on just as she had done before. There was also something different about his physical features: his eyes seemed to have become enlarged and fiery. He never looked at you when he was talking, but stared past you in an empty vacant manner as if he was talking to someone beyond you and not to you.

Martina was called back to the present, when Leonie who had asked a question and gotten no reply, shouted in her ears. She jumped and apologized for having gone into the world at home. Leonie told her that she should stop burdening herself with everybody else's problem or else she would become old in her teenage years.

That afternoon as they entered the classroom, they could hear the students talking excitedly. They both wondered aloud what had happened. As soon as they entered the classroom, the talking ceased as if by a pre-arranged or rehearsed signal. The girls looked around to see if the teacher who was supposed to teach at the time was behind them but he was not. They went to their seats and as soon as Martina sat, she observed a piece of paper on her desk. She knew she had tidied her desk before she went for lunch and wondered who had put it there. Their form teacher Mrs. Lyn had warned them about littering their work area or the classroom as this was an indication of nastiness which would not be tolerated.

Martina picked up the paper and looked at it. Someone had made a graphic drawing of her swimming in a pool. She appeared to be using only one hand as the other hand was pulling along a large string bag. There were drawings of hundred dollar bills, cellular phones, a calculator and a Rolex watch. In the pool there were different military figures, a policeman and two soldiers chasing her with guns poised. Martina made a grunt and tears blurred her vision. This could not be related to her in any way! The graphic drawing needed no explanation and the words written in bold type TIEFING GHETTO GAL! did not fail to further the accusation.

Martina felt like how Christ must have felt on the cross; injured, cheated, a skeletal frame without flesh and blood, wronged, an object of dire cruelty! She had never stolen anything at school and had not been tempted to. Her biggest problem had been hunger, hunger for food but not hunger for material things. Moreover, if she had stolen all those items she would have to stash them somewhere far from home because her mother did not condone wrong-doing and would have peeled her skin from her body if she ever found out that she had stolen anything from anyone. She had often warned them of certain people's perception of inner-city people. They were all supposed to be illiterate, thieves, murderers, idlers, non-achievers and anything derogatory that the human mind could perceive. She had always told her that opportunities were limited for them and many did not achieve because of their attitude and lack of help, but she should try and hold up her head because if she held it down too much, she would fall flat on her face and eat dirt. She thought of how hungry she was at times and if she had stolen all those items she would have sold them and gotten money to buy food.

She heard, without looking up, the scraping of the chairs and desks and knew that the teacher had arrived for the class. She knew that she should stand but could not move from the chair. The teacher came in and stood for a while, waiting for her to stand. The students followed her eyes and when they realized that Martina was the reason for their having to stand for so long, they started calling out to her.

The boy sitting closest to her said, "Girl you blind or what? You don't see the teacher in the classroom?"

Martina rose slowly, keeping her head down, not daring to lift her eyes. Her nose burned with embarrassment and she was fighting hard to keep the tears from betraying her. She gratefully sat when they were told to do so and for the whole class she did not internalize anything. The teacher's voice intruded into her thoughts a few times but the isolated words made no real mental contact.

At the end of school she rushed home without even talking to Leonie or going to her swimming lesson. She could hardly eat that evening, the food tasted like paste but she forced it down her throat because hunger pains were teasing her ribs, poking fingers here and there. She went to bed early that evening instead of reading a novel as she usually did after doing her homework. Sleep avoided her in the early hours and kept its distance until the old day was ready to bid goodbye.

The next day when she arrived at school, she waited close to the gate for Leonie to arrive. For some reason, she dreaded going into the classroom. While she was standing there, quite a number of students passing by stared at her in a curious and questioning manner. She was not a fool and assumed right away that news of her being a thief had winged its way around the school or maybe a part of the school. She felt uncomfortable at the unwelcome attention and was walking away when she heard somebody calling her name. She turned around and saw Tian and the girl that she closely resembled walking towards her. When they were right beside her, Tian stopped but the girl flounced right pass, holding her head straight.

"Why weren't you at practice yesterday?" asked Tian.

"I wasn't feeling well and had to rush home," replied Martina with a lie, too embarrassed to tell the truth.

"Well, in the future you need to inform the teacher as too many absences from practice without the teacher's permission could cause you to lose your coveted spot on the team."

"Thanks for the advice Tian, I'll be sure to bear that in mind."

Martina was moving away to class when Leonie came up beside her.

"Why the hasty exit yesterday, you didn't even stop to tell me bye, and why were you so upset in class?" enquired Leonie.

Martina told her what had happened, omitting the words written on the piece of paper. Leonie was aghast and expressed shocked surprise.

"But when those things were stolen you wasn't even anywhere near those students! Moreover you and I are mostly together and during P.E. time and other times we are mostly with the rest of the class and not alone in the classroom!"

They both wondered who had started the rumour and why. As they walked towards the classroom Martina counted at least thrice that she had heard the word 't'ief' as she walked pass different groups of children. Martina tried to remain calm but Leonie declared that she was going to curse anyone who uttered the word thief within her hearing again.

Things grew worse when they went into their classroom. Some of the students visibly withdrew themselves as Martina came near to or walked pass them. As soon as they passed, they turned to stare at her in an accusing manner, their faces expressing disgust and outrage. Martina and Leonie pretended not to notice and continued a stilted conversation. They went to Martina's seat and both of them sat on the chair. Leonie knew that her friend needed a friend at that time and had made up her mind to support her in whatever way she could. As they sat down, a sheet of paper, again with drawing and words, greeted them. The person had cleverly pasted it to the desk so that it could not blow away before Martina saw it. This time the drawing showed a ragged person clutching the items stolen in the class. The words bawling out at her in bold black writing were:

GO HOME TIEFING GHETTO GAL TINA

Martina tried to tear it from the desk before Leonie could internalize it, but Leonie held her hand and told her not to destroy it because she might need it for evidence. Martina wondered what evidence she was talking about. All that she cared about was destroying any form of accusation or ridicule aimed at her. Leonie took the paper from her, folded it and handed it back to her, admonishing her not to destroy it. She hugged her friend tightly, whispering to her that everything would be sorted out and that she should not cry as that would give her enemies more to talk about. Martina had no intention of crying. Crying happened because the soft human part of a person was hurt and sad and needed an outlet to display the hurt and sadness. Hurt and sad she certainly felt, but the soft human part of her existed no more. She felt cold and callous. Revenge took over her being as she pushed the cautioning voices of her mother, Miss Turner, her primary school teacher and everyone else who had spoken against revenge to the bottom of her mind. She knew what she was going to do to the next person who called her a thief.

The morning classes came to an end and soon it was time for break. She really didn't feel like going outside but Leonie asked her to accompany her to the bathroom, and not really wanting to be left by herself in the classroom, Martina decided to accompany her. She walked behind Leonie and just as they got to the front of the classroom someone stretched a foot into her way and quite audibly said the word 't'ief'. Martina almost fell on her face and used her hands to break her fall just in time. She stood up firmly and then directed a calm, cold stare to her tormentor. She could recognize that voice anywhere. It was scornful and filled with pride and venom. She reached out and grabbed Stone Cold.

All the taunting, scorn, evil comments and spiteful actions that had been flung at her for the three years overpowered

Martina's mind. Coldness took over and even when she heard the harsh sound of fabric being torn, she did not release Stone Cold. Instead, she flung her to the wall and started hitting her, first in her face as she held her with one hand and then all over her body as she released her and started using both hands. Stone Cold had been taken completely by surprise. She had no idea of what was happening until she found herself against the wall being hit. She tried to fight back and being the stouter of the two by far, should have been able to put down Martina quite easily but could not. She got in a few feeble hits but they made no impression whatever on the cold enraged Martina who seemed to have lost control and was dodging most of Stone Cold's frightened blows and delivering them back forcefully at the same time.

Some of the children in the class started screaming. They were so frightened that none of them tried to stop the fight. A few of the girls ran off to seek help and Leonie and three boys who seemed to have been shaken out of shock came forward and tried to part the fighting pair who were by now on the floor locked in a fierce struggle, both trying to push the other off. The four tried to pull apart the fighting pair, but it was like trying to free something which had become stuck with crazy glue. Other children joined in and managed to tear them apart but not before one received a blow to the face which sent him reeling across the classroom and landing him on top of a desk to the great amusement of those who had not volunteered to stop the fight.

The children who had gone to get the teachers returned with two of them, one male and a female. The teachers each grabbed one of the fighters. Stone Cold was holding the front of her uniform and was bawling as if a loved one had died. Her whole face had turned red and looked swollen in some areas. Her right eye was swollen and had an abrasion coming out of the lashes. As she bawled, her whole body shook and she managed to form the words "I must kill you. Wait and see!" The teachers told her to shut up and behave herself. Martina just looked at her cold and unmoved, and calmly told her to go ahead.

Martina did not seem to be much affected. The only signs of the fight she had just engaged in were a bruise on her left cheek and a dishevelled appearance. There were no tears and her calm, composed exterior did not betray the feeling of panic which had crept over her now that the fight was over. She knew that she was in trouble for fighting at school. She knew her mother would probably beat her and she knew that Miss Turner and her swimming teacher would be saddened by what she had done. She tried to reason that Stone Cold deserved what she had got. She had tried hard for three years to ignore her but the girl had kept on maligning her. She felt remorse for those she had disappointed, but did not regret trouncing Miss Vanity Pride.

Her form teacher and the principal behaved as if the girls were on their way to be hanged and repeatedly told them to pray for their sins and pray about the disgraceful manner in which they had behaved as females. The principal likened them to the proverbial fish vendors and threatened to expel both of them if they ever committed even the slightest misdemeanour. He asked each of the fighters and two other witnesses from the class to write an account about the fight. At the end of the session, the fighters went home with a letter summoning a parent or guardian who should be present at the school not later than eight o'clock the following day.

When Martina got home that afternoon, she went to Miss Turner's house instead of hers. Even though she knew that Miss Turner would be hurt by her behaviour, she felt that it would be better to talk to her before handing the letter to her mother. When she knocked on Miss Turner's door, she opened it and told Martina that her mother was at home. She sat beside Martina and started to question her. At first, Martina sat silently and sadly, not responding to the questions, staring off into another world instead. Miss Turner pulled her back to the present by telling her that whatever was wrong was not going to be made right by running away from it. She thought about it and decided that it was true. She told Miss Turner the whole story from the beginning and then ended with the fight. When she was through, the words of rebuke and remonstration she had expected did not come. She looked at Miss Turner in a bewildered manner, wondering if she had heard or fully understood what she had told her, especially about fighting.

Miss Turner did something strange; she put her arms around Martina, hugging her for a long while without saying anything. Then she got up and told her not to move from where she was sitting. She did not go into her house but to Martina's house instead. She heard voices coming from the house but the words were indistinct. She wondered what her mother was saying and whether she would be punished. After waiting for an interminable period, the two women came out of the house. Martina stood up, ready to run inside her house and take whatever was coming to her, instead of allowing the whole lane to view her being punished. Miss Fuller saw her standing and told her to sit. She did so warily, wondering what they were up to. They sat on both sides of her and she felt like the filling of a sandwich, unable to breathe, ready to be devoured.

All three of them sat in silence as if contemplating a serious step. Her mother was the first to speak and when she did her words startled Martina.

"Reada, Miss Turner tell me what happen at school and what happening there for a long time now."

She paused as if she was going through the discomfort and pain Martina had gone through.

"I don't agree with fighting. It don't get rid of the problem. See what happen between Shim an' me. The fight make things worse! A can't even talk to my own son. A lost him, an' it hurt me bad bad."

There were tears in her voice and she was finding it difficult to talk. She stopped speaking for a while and Martina almost forgot her own troubles as her heart reached out to her. She could empathize with her because of what she had gone through and moreover she was a member of the family.

"A fight with him because him ways did hurt me and I suppose is the same t'ing with you and this girl. A not swearing for you but a know you don't trouble people an' a know you not a t'ief! None a them have any right to call you a t'ief! A not giving you any right to fight but maybe a would have done the same thing. Telling lie on people especially about serious t'ings like stealing is a evilous thing. A not even going to ask you if you steal those things because although a can't swear a know is not you."

Her voice had risen and Miss Turner quickly tapped her on the thigh and said, "Don't talk so loud, we don't want to tell the whole lane our business."

Miss Fuller lowered her voice and continued, "A want you to come out to something good in life. A don't want you to be anything at all like me. You hear, don't follow anything at all that I do." Her voice had a pleading quality to it. It was almost as if she was on her knees, praying. Martina wondered if she was making reference to her three children by three different fathers, her nightly sojourn to wherever and her inability to adequately provide for her family. Well she didn't have to beg that hard, Martina thought, because she had no intention of being like her mother. She resolved to fight with all she had to avoid the poverty stricken lifestyle. She continued to speak, breaking into Martina's thoughts.

"A know that some rich, white looking people don't want to have anything to do with the likes of us. But this world is a big place and have enough space for all the different race of people that God make – black, white, yellow, red and all the ones that don't know where they belong, like the girl you fight with at school. Don't let anybody make you feel less than what you are. Work hard and do your best and even though I not a Christian but God must help you one way or the other."

She spent quite a long time talking to Martina, begging her to do well and pleading with her not to fight again although there were times in life when one had no choice. The talk which she gave that afternoon was the longest and most sober talk that Martina had ever heard from her. She felt that she understood her mother a little better even though she did not explain certain things in her life.

The next day Martina's mother accompanied her to Milverton. She wished she had not chosen to wear that short red dress. The only good thing about it was that apart from partially exposing her thighs, everywhere else was covered. Martina hated the red boots she wore with it and wished she could have worn something more conventional. The biggest blessing was that she had not put on the red wig. Most of the clothes she wore were always complimented by a matching wig. Instead of the wig, she wore a red bandoo and scrunchie in her finely braided hair.

As they sat silently in the foyer, Stone Cold and her mother walked in. She was a white woman. Martina suspected that Stone Cold's father must be a Negro or had claims to Negro blood because Stone Cold did not look exactly white. Stone Cold touched her mother and lifted her chin in Martina and her mother's direction. The mother looked across at them in a hostile manner and met a similar gaze. The eyes stared into one another and Stone Cold's mother was the first to look away. Martina noted that she had a surly look which she had most definitely passed on to her daughter. She was wearing a cream linen pants suit which was made to accentuate her large breasts and hips. The expensive suit was complimented by burgundy leather pumps and hand bag. To complete the outfit there were the car keys dangling from her hands which she kept shaking as if she was nervous. Martina knew that she was going to put up quite a defence for her daughter. She was not looking forward to what was to come.

At eight fifteen, both pairs were ushered into the principal's spacious air-conditioned office. There were several landscape paintings which cheered up the dull green wall. They were offered seats on leather chairs. The principal greeted them in a sombre tone and announced that before they could commence, the lower school vice principal, guidance counsellor, the girls' form teacher and the swimming instructor had to be present. During the next five minutes they all arrived and the meeting started.

The principal began by reading the rule pertaining to fights from the rule book. After reading the rule he read the penalty two times, enunciating the words and taking as much pains as if he was a judge pronouncing a verdict and explaining why it had to be so. He then gave a summary of the fight as it had been reported, and asked the form teacher to read the reports written by the two girls and two witnesses. He then asked Stone Cold to tell her story and before she started, he warned both girls to speak the truth.

Stone Cold told her story, omitting all the rude things she had done to Martina. As a matter of fact, she did not mention the grade seven and eight years, but the immediate incident which had landed them in the principal's office. She said she had not called Martina a thief but that the word had been used because there had been a discussion on the rumour which had been circulated that Martina was the person who had been stealing the items in the class. When the vice principal asked her how she had come by the news she said she was not sure as quite a number of students had been discussing it. She denied sticking out her foot in the aisle on purpose and said she might have stuck it out simply to stretch it just as Martina was passing by.

Martina listened without saying a word, waiting for her time to come to tell her side of the story. Her mother had warned her against butting in when someone else was speaking. As soon as Stone Cold was finished, Martina was instructed to speak. She did not begin at the fight but at the grade seven year and the shoes episode. When she got to the notes, she was asked to produce them, but could only produce the second one as she had destroyed the first. Everyone present except Stone Cold and her mother were shocked. Stone Cold's mother defended her daughter by pointing out that she was not an artist and could not possibly have drawn the picture on the paper. She appealed to them to ask the Art and Craft teacher to testify to this, and the guidance counsellor said that this could be verified.

The principal was very unhappy about the teasing; Martina attributed this to the "Mango Dive" and almost smiled in spite of the seriousness of the situation. He pointed out that it was not a good thing to tease anyone, especially about situations that they were unable to do anything about. He told them that when he was growing up in the rural area he went to school barefooted as the one pair of shoes he had was only for dressing occasions such as going to church or other special functions. He pointed out that he was not taking sides but knew exactly how Martina felt. He wrote down the names of students who could corroborate the two girls' stories and announced their names on the intercom, asking them to report at once to the office.

Leonie and Stone Cold's friend told their stories after which they were subjected to cross questioning. After they were sent back to their classes, the principal summed up the case, ascribing blame to both girls. If one listened keenly, it could be gleaned that there was sympathy in his voice for Martina. He spoke directly to each parent about her special role in bringing up children, especially girls, to show respect for one another and not to fight when things could be solved otherwise. He referred them both for counselling and asked the guidance counsellor to set up times to accommodate them. They were each suspended for three days. Martina's mother protested this quite vehemently, pointing out that it was clear her child had been wronged and had only defended herself. The principal pointed out that while this might be true, both girls had broken the school rule and had to be punished accordingly.

Martina and her mother left with her mother still protesting the harsh sentence. Mrs. Stone said nothing but her face did not betray what she was thinking. Martina was especially worried about missing her classes, but her swimming instructor promised to get the homework to her somehow. Martina was glad that she did not tell her that she couldn't be on the swimming team anymore.

Twelve

Martina entered the bus and sat in one of the middle seats. It was the first morning of her grade ten year and she was filled with anxious expectancy as to what upper school would entail. She had been warned by the principal and other teachers at the meeting she had attended with her mother that the fun and frolic was over, and serious work in preparation for the Caribbean Examination Council (CXC) would begin in earnest. The principal pointed out that in essence, the work had started since grade seven but the last two years, grades ten and eleven, were to be used to hone the skills and knowledge gleaned earlier, and to pursue the courses at a more advanced level. He warned that those who wasted their grade ten year would not be sent up for any examination by the school, even if the parents pleaded and cried, or offered to pay a million dollars.

Martina had chosen basically Art subjects. She had been placed in a special group with other students who were doing ten subjects instead of the normal eight. In addition to the compulsory subjects, English Language and Mathematics, she had chosen Spanish, French, History, English Literature, Geography, Computer Science, Social Science and Biology. She shied away from the Business options because she felt she had no aptitude for this.

Despite her partially troubled year in grade nine, she had still managed to do well. She had stayed away for a whole week at one time and several single days when she had no money for school. She had to use sickness as an excuse. Leonie had kept her up to date with all the readings and assignments and she had managed to keep up her average. She knew she was in for an even harder year because her mother's so called flu had worsened. Sometimes for two whole days she did not get out of bed. She noticed though that she still went out a few nights but not half as much as she used to. She was very pleased at Martina's progress and told her so. She encouraged her to work even harder because she wanted her to get a good job when she left school.

Martina had a problem with working right after she left school as she interpreted leaving school to mean right after grade eleven. She had often looked on and admired the sixth formers. They were the academic giants of the school. Being in sixth form meant one had done well in CXC and had demonstrated the ability to go on to tertiary level work. Martina had always seen herself moving up to that level. She didn't want to work after grade eleven; she wanted to be among the sixth formers. She didn't want a job in a store or in an office answering the telephone or typing; she hated typing. She wanted a profession, not just an ordinary job. The way she figured it, if she got herself properly qualified, even though she was from the inner-city, no one could deny her a job. She had no idea how she would ever get money for further education but that did not stop her aspirations. Furthermore, she wanted to help her family. Her mother was obviously ill and needed help and she wanted to help her brother and sister and Miss Turner.

For the first time she was wearing a very good pair of shoes befitting Milverton High and carrying a brand name bag, compliments of Miss Turner. Her brother had brought her the two uniforms she had. She was accustomed to him giving her a little money now and again, but when he had come in one night, a week before the opening of school, and had given her the money and the uniforms, she was both surprised and glad. She knew her mother was having even more serious financial problems than usual as she had to be spending money to get treatment for the stubborn flu. Yvette had received her two uniforms from her but Martina had not received any. The last one from grade nine had been in such a bad condition that she knew she could not possibly wear it back to school. Her school fee had been paid as usual by the Member of Parliament and her mother had bought the books she needed for grade ten.

She was feeling very good about school but otherwise she was gravely troubled. No matter how hard she tried, where she went and what she did, she could not get Yvette out of her mind. The thought of Yvette rested on her mind like heavy fog after rain in a hilly area. This fog made everything else in her mind obscure and when she tried to get out of the fog, it entangled her more, not wanting her to find a way out.

At the beginning of the previous summer holiday, Yvette's father had arrived at the house and made an unusual request. Instead of giving Martina's mother the monthly allowance and leaving as he normally did, he told her that all his mother's grandchildren were going abroad to spend the holidays with other relatives. As a result of that she would be left alone with the helper and needed to have a little company, somebody to read to her and go to the shop. He pointed out that she would be enjoying a lifestyle she had never had before and that she would be well fed and taken care of.

Yvette did not want to go. She liked the idea of spending time in a lovely house with her own room and bathroom, but living among strangers did not really appeal to her. She would have no one of her own age to speak to and she did not know what she would do on her own or how to act around elderly people. Moreover, the place was far and she could not get to run home if things went wrong. She was very reluctant to go but her father insisted and threatened not to give her any more money. Yvette's mother had wondered at the strange request and had asked the father bluntly why the sudden interest. He pointed out that the child also belonged to him and could go to his family anytime he wanted her to. She told him he only wanted to use the child because there was no one else to use. They argued loud and long but the father had his way and the next weekend a very subdued and sorrowful looking Yvette left with her father. When she got into his van, she stayed so close to the door that one got the impression that she would jump out at any time.

The visit lasted for three weeks, two weeks less than the time the father had said she would stay. Martina missed her very much and for the first time realized that she loved her sparkling sister very much. Even though her friend from her old primary school came to visit her and she also went to visit her friend a few times, she was lonely. There was no one to argue with or tell to be quiet. Martina was glad that she had borrowed some novels to read and spent most of her time reading.

One day, three weeks after Yvette left, Martina was outside in the backyard hanging up some clothes when she heard something which sounded like a vehicle at her gate. Out of curiosity, she peeped around the corner of the house and saw a red Isuzu motor car. It had stopped right by her gate and she was curious to see who it was. The back door was pushed open hastily and Yvette stepped out of the car. As Martina watched, Yvette pushed back her body into the car and came out with two bags, one which she had taken with her and one which Martina had never seen before. She started walking as fast as she could, which was not very fast, considering the weight of the two bags. Before she had gotten very far she stopped and turned towards the car. A man, who closely resembled her father came out of the car and spoke to her. After listening for a little while, she stomped off, opened the gate and came through without looking back at the man. The man watched her until she got to the door but made no move to accompany her. He shouted something which sounded like 'Remember' to Yvette who did not hear or pretended not to hear as she did not respond in any way.

Martina rushed around the front of the house shouting out Yvette's name. Yvette did not answer; Martina thought she was playing as she sometimes did. She was expecting her to turn around and shout in her face but Yvette only turned around when Martina yanked her blouse from behind.

When Yvette turned around, Martina just stood and stared at her as if she was a strange being or as if someone had reduced her to a log standing upright. The eyes that met hers for a few seconds and then looked away had a faint hint of the former Yvette's eyes, but something was missing because Yvette could outstare anyone she wanted to at anytime. Yvette was known to be precocious or as Jamaicans would put it, she was 'dry eye'. Martina was puzzled, not only was Yvette not holding her gaze for long but her face looked thin and sad like a starving stray animal. Martina held her by the shoulder and forced her to look at her.

"Yvette," she said in alarm, "what happened to you? Did they beat you or treat you bad?" Yvette did not answer. Yvette who always had a cutting retort for almost everything, loud, talkative Yvette who always had to be told to tone down and be quiet, now was not saying a word. Her eyes looked as if she was a frightened baby animal ready to spring away, afraid of everyone but its mother.

Martina grew alarmed and shook Yvette. "What is wrong with you? Are you sick? What happen, dem beat you? Talk to me and stop pretendin' like you can't talk! What happen? You getting mad?"

"Martina a want to sleep," were her words, spoken very softly as if she did not even want to hear her own voice or was apologizing for speaking at all.

Martina was shocked, Yvette had called her Martina, like a stranger would. Something was really wrong. She held Yvette and gently pushed her inside the house, and then she went back outside for the two bags and then closed the door behind them. Their mother and brother were not at home and Martina did not know what to do. Yvette had climbed on the bed they shared, turned her back and pulled up her legs. Without thinking, Martina climbed on the bed, lay behind her and put her arms around her. She did not turn or speak and Martina could hear her breathing heavily.

She did not know how long they lay like that because the next thing she knew was that her mother was calling to her and asking why she had gone to bed so early and forgotten to lock the door properly. She launched off into a lecture about all the things that could have happened but stopped midway in her third sentence when she saw the form of somebody else on the bed. She asked Martina which of her friends was sleeping over without her permission and seemed stunned but happy when Martina told her that it was Yvette. She demanded to know why no one had informed her that Yvette was coming back before time and asked when she had come. Martina answered her question and then told her that something was wrong with Yvette. As soon as she made the statement, Miss Fuller ran over to the bed and asked Martina what she meant. Martina tried to explain, but words deserted her.

Miss Fuller sat on the bed and shook Yvette as if she was afraid she was dead and wanted to bring her back to life. She did not stop until Yvette responded with a scream, asking to be left alone. Miss Fuller got her into a sitting position and told her that she was going to pour some water on her if she did not wake up quickly and start talking. This threat did not move Yvette to speak. She opened her eyes and looked around as if she wanted to bolt. Miss Fuller spoke very loudly to her but to all her questions, Yvette answered one word "nothing".

Martina's mother sent her to call Miss Turner at once. When she arrived, she stared strangely at Yvette and after looking at her and trying to speak to her; she declared that a ghost must have touched her or played with her and had therefore harmed her. She recounted a number of stories where this had happened when she was a young person growing up in the country. She made some suggestions as to what should be done but none of them entailed taking her to the doctor. Martina did not believe in the ghost invasion story. She thought something else must be wrong and had traumatised the girl, but when she put the idea forward it was rejected on the grounds that she was too young to understand those matters and that she read too much and what was happening was not one of the stories from her novels.

Miss Fuller decided that she was going to call the father to get some information about how evil had taken hold of her child. At the mention of the father, Yvette held on to her hand and shouted no. When her mother asked her why, she raised her frightened face and with large petrified eyes, shouted no again. She even held on to her mother's hand as if to deter her. When her mother saw the torment on her face she broke into tears. All three of them cried. Martina was not only crying for

Yvette but for her mother who seemed to be getting sicker each day, and in addition to that, had to face the new problem with Yvette.

Miss Turner and Yvette's mother eventually took her to Clarendon to get help from a renowned obeah woman. They had a difficult time getting her into the taxi that day as she fought and cried. Martina looked on in tears but refused to be drawn in the obeah trip. She had voiced the opinion that the involvement of a mother woman was ancient foolishness and would end up doing more harm than good. She pointed out that Yvette was improving because even though she spoke very little and refused most of the times to play with or be with her friends, her face looked less petrified and she had started eating a little. Her mother conceded that this might be so, but pointed out that she could not attend school in the condition she was in, so the ghost must be exorcised. Martina had read about exorcisms a number of times and did not want to be a witness to it. She wished she could save Yvette from that superstitious garbage, but as a child her words went unheeded like a cry for help made in a tumultuous storm.

When Yvette came back there was no change. She stuck close to Martina and had even more nightmares. She often screamed out, "No, leave me!" The mother woman had confirmed that she was beset by a ghost and an East Indian one called a coolie duppy. Miss Fuller believed her because even though she knew very little about Yvette's father side of the family, she knew that there were people of Indian descent in it. The woman had told her that it would take a little time to leave her and had given them a number of bottles with various oils to rub her and had instructed that she should sleep in something red each night. Martina could not help laughing at the stupidity of the whole thing. She marvelled that in the twenty first century when people were trying to shield themselves from bullets, her mother was trying to shield her sister from a ghost. She wondered if Yvette's Indian ghost had been a farmer or a gunman.

As she travelled to school she wondered what would happen to Yvette at school. Would she be able to learn? Would the teachers be cross with her when she did not respond to them? Would any of the students want to be her friend? She wished she could be with her to help her in some way.

Shimron, even though he seemed not to be a part of the family sometimes, took the whole thing badly. From the look on his face, whenever he was at home and stood or sat scrutinizing Yvette, one could see the questioning look of sadness on his face. When he had been told of the problem, he had agreed with Martina that no ghost was responsible for Yvette's condition. Knowing that his mother would not welcome his opinion, he reserved it, and spoke his thoughts only to Martina. She noticed that he would bring little gifts for Yvette and even tried to get her to talk to him. Martina was pleased that at least he showed some interest. She could see that their mother felt good about it too even though she said nothing.

Martina was perplexed by Yvette's father's behaviour. He had been to the house two times since Yvette's strange illness but did not come inside the house or speak to Yvette in any way. His visits did not last more than five minutes as he fled as soon as Miss Fuller started lambasting him for taking her child away and causing his evil duppies to possess her and then dumping the problem on her. Martina observed that he did not dispute the ghost possession story or put forward any logical explanation as to what was wrong with Yvette. Martina also observed that Yvette had become almost hysterical the two times when he came around. She refused to get out of the house and spoke to no one after he had left. When Martina hugged her and tried to comfort her, she tried to fight her off and would end up sobbing on her shoulder.

CR꣸CR꣸

Martina entered her new classroom and prayed that her perpetual foe, Stone Cold, would not be in her class. She knew that this was a futile wish because if the truth was to be told, Stone Cold was a brilliant girl and had always done well. When she looked at the list posted in the classroom, her heart fell because Helenetta Stone's name was there, written as boldly as all the other names. She did not attend school for the first week and Martina learnt that she was ill and would not turn up before the next week. Since the fight, she stayed as far away as possible from Martina, and every time Martina caught her looking at her, she swiftly averted her gaze. Martina knew that she was sizzling with rage at the trouncing she had received, but dared not tease or interfere with her. Everyone looked upon her as a force to be wary of and for the most part left her to herself. She was pleased when she saw Leonie and Hairnet's name on the list. She felt that at least she would have two people to talk to.

As the week progressed, she realized that if she was going to keep in line with the work, she had to be very attentive, be very prompt with her assignments and put out as much effort as she could. She found she could not sit musing about her personal problems but had to clear her thoughts and become focused and adopt a positive attitude to all the different subject areas. She had no intention of failing any, even though the sciences were going to offer her a challenge.

School now ended after three-o-clock every day of the week and then she had swimming for three afternoons. She knew she had to work out a way to balance both areas because she was determined that none of them would suffer. The swimming teacher had told her that she was improving and if she continued she would be able to try out for the national team in the next two years or so. Martina did not share this news with anyone but secretly harboured the dream that one day she would represent her country and then everyone would see that people from the inner-city could do as well as people from other upper social levels. Her specialties were the breaststroke and the butterfly, especially the butterfly. She often imagined herself to be a butterfly, free and beautiful, flitting from one place to the other and creating a colourful, pleasant view to the beholders. The only thing she did not like about the butterfly was its delicate appearance. In her life, delicacy was a negative factor, not a positive one. If she was going to achieve her aspirations, she would have to be aggressive and assertive, not in an unpleasant manner but in standing up for herself and relentlessly forging ahead in managing her school and home affairs. She did not want to be a cliché or hackneyed example of an inner-city girl. She wanted to battle against the forces of poverty, low social status and the expectations of those who had passed the law that achievement for her kind was not attainable.

At first, Martina was not certain what she wanted to pursue as a career but over a year now it had entered her mind that Mass Communication was what she wanted to do. At the Career Exposition which had taken place in her grade nine year, she had learnt that in order for one to be successful in such a career, one had to have a good grasp of the English Language, be able to write and speak lucidly and be knowledgeable of public affairs. During the past holiday, she had spent some time trying to write a few short stories and poems. At first she had tried to write about ideas she had picked up from her readings but discovered that the ideas came very slowly and as soon as she had written a few paragraphs she would come to a standstill.

One day, a group of young men living in the lane had an altercation. Martina was coming from swimming when it started and as she was afraid to pass them, she had taken refuge in Miss Tit's shop with some other people who were also afraid to go out into the road. It was an exposed secret that the young men were carriers of guns and no one wanted to be shot. The fight had ended with one man being stabbed in the left arm.

When Martina tried to write again, she thought of the fight and started writing about it. She filled in background ideas and descriptions and found out that she could write several pages about what had happened in her community. She had decided over the holiday to become a member of the Writers' Club and the Debating Club, but both were held on the same afternoon. She decided that she was going to alternate in attending those clubs and was glad that they were not held on the same afternoon as her swimming classes. If she had any intention in considering Mass Communication, she realized that as introverted as she was, she had to pull out of herself and learn to speak publicly.

It was at the Debating Club that she made a new friend. When she first went to the club, she sat at the back of the classroom feeling lost and lonely. The Debating Coordinator was her English teacher, Miss Miller. When she saw Martina, she welcomed her specially and told her that she was glad she was interested in other important things besides swimming. When she mentioned swimming all heads turned to look at Martina. She wanted to make herself inconspicuous but did not know how to. The teacher asked every one to introduce his or herself. She also asked them to name their class and their career path. She pointed out to them that the skills they would learn in the club would prove to be invaluable and would be assets in every facet of their academic and social life. She gave examples of this and then moved on to outline terms and strategies used in debating. Martina found the whole session very interesting and decided that she would really like to be involved in the activities.

At the end of the meeting, Martina took up her bag and headed for the door. She found her path blocked by the grade eleven boy who had asked the teacher some really interesting questions during the club meeting. Martina asked to be excused and when her request was denied, she found herself straining her neck slightly upwards to look questioningly into a narrow, straight face with black mischievous eyes, dark shadowy moustache and the beginnings of a beard. There were a number of bumps residing on his cocoa brown complexioned forehead. Martina was sure that he was over six feet tall and labelled him right away as one of the basketballers. Despite his narrow face, he was big-bodied and Martina thought he was quite easily over two hundred pounds. He was not really handsome but was attractive if one paid attention to his mischievous smile and shadowy moustache.

Martina said to the bulk blocking her,

"Could you kindly excuse me?"

She tried to sound stern but her sternness must have amused him because he laughed loudly and remained where he was standing much to the annoyance of those who were standing at the door waiting to come out. When he realized that he was blocking others, he shifted to the side. Martina seized the opportunity to go her way but had taken only a few steps when she realized that he was following her. The basketballers thought that they were the most important persons in the school and were always trying to engage all the girls' attention. Martina had a big problem with people who were popular because they always thought that they were extending a favour to anyone they spoke to and behaved as if one was supposed to be in obeisance to them. Well, she did not know what this one wanted and she was not going to acknowledge him.

He fell in step with her and greeted her, "Hi Martina. You are certainly in a hurry. Are you going swimming?"

"Yes, I am in a hurry to get home. Do you mind my doing so?" she said with indifference, hoping that this would make him stop following her.

"It's not that late. Why are you hurrying so much?" he asked, oblivious to her indifference.

"It might be early for you, but it's late for me," she retorted. "What do you want any way?"

"I thought you would never ask. I would like to make your acquaintance. My name is Andre Depass, captain of the basketball team. I always watch you swim. If you continue you are going to be really good."

Martina thought that this was a strange young man. Most of the boys she knew would never say that they wanted to make your acquaintance; they would whistle at you or call to you in a rude way and hope you would respond. She thought he must be from one of those old fashioned families where chivalry persisted. But even as she thought this, she knew that if one of his friends was present he would never have spoken to her like that, because he would be scornfully ridiculed. She wondered if he was trying to impress her and for what. Boys normally had some hidden motive when they were so friendly. As if he was psychic and had read her thoughts, he explained, "I like the company of brilliant, athletic girls, especially those who are not loud and proud."

Martina thought to herself that he had gotten the last two adjectives right, but she wasn't certain about the first two.

"Well, I am certain you have made a mistake because I am not brilliant or athletic."

He laughed and she was sure his eyes were playing around mischievously as he said, "At this school only brilliant students are allowed to do ten subjects and if you were not athletic you would not be able to swim so fast."

"Well, you seem to have all the answers so I need not provide you with any," Martina replied, walking faster.

"You certainly are in a hurry Martina. Is your parent here to pick you up?" asked Andre.

"No, I take the bus to and from school," Martina replied emphatically. Maybe when he found out that she was not one of the wealthy students, he would quickly unmake her acquaintance. But her answer did not seem to bother him as he continued to talk. As they neared the gate he looked around as if searching to see whether his ride had come or not. He then said to her, "Maybe I can offer you a ride. Where do you live?"

He had asked the dreaded question. Martina did not like to be asked where she lived and had never really told anyone but Leonie (and that was only the year before) where she lived.

She avoided doing this because she knew the reaction and the looks that her reply would gender. She didn't really care what Andre thought, but at the same time she was not about to tell him.

"I do not live anywhere," she said. "You are certainly not going my way!"

He certainly had not picked up any underlying meaning because all he said was, "You are certainly living up to your brilliance. Never take rides from strangers, that's what every mother tells every girl. Well Martina from nowhere, see you around and I certainly will!"

He walked away and she went to the bus stop wondering about this strange, seemingly mannerly young man. Her mother kept making comments about her being fifteen and learning to hold up her head. She had warned her about males in general and how they liked to fool young girls. She told Martina that she should never allow herself to be numbered among the girls who had dropped out of school. She told her that everyone was counting on her to hold up her head. She watched her like a cat waiting to pounce on an unsuspecting lizard and rarely sent her anywhere. Martina knew that if she knew that the boys in the lane were always trying to entice her into relationships with them she would certainly threaten to kill all of them.

Martina thought she was worrying herself unduly and told her so. She knew her mother was suffering physically and with Yvette's problem added to their poverty, she knew her mother would literally die if she fell by the way. Although Martina did not voice it, she knew her mother was afraid that what had befallen her would also befall her. Her mother had given birth to Shimron when she was only fifteen and she was trying her best not to let that happen to her children.

Well, Martina resolved to herself, *I will not let that happen. My life may turn out to be broken and sad but if I have my way it will not be because of pregnancy.*

As she stood by the bus stop, a car braked suddenly on the other side and a wide-eyed lady fixed her with a long stare. Martina wondered if she thought that she was the girl who closely resembled her and stared back at her in return. After about a minute, the woman shook her head and drove away.

Thirteen

Martina jumped out of bed in a frightened manner. It was almost seven o'clock and no one had woken her up. Yvette was still sleeping beside her and Shimron's bed was still neat, suggesting he had not come in at all. Her mother's bedroom door was still locked, and Martina did not bother to wake her. She grabbed her toiletries and clothes and rushed to the kitchen, hurriedly bathed, put on her clothes and collected her books. It was only when she realized that she had no lunch money that she knocked on her mother's room door and without waiting for an answer, she pushed herself in. Her mother woke up at the sound and asked Martina what time it was. She told her mother and asked for her lunch money. She dashed outside, bag on her back and a small folder with a project in her hand.

It was only when she had stepped outside that she realized that it was raining slightly. Martina decided that it was not heavy enough for her to unearth the lopsided umbrella which closely resembled Mad Bee's old hut which leant precariously to one side and would one day certainly collapse. All attempts to remove Mad Bee from her house had proven futile as she seemed to be always awake and threw any missile available at anyone who tried to enter her premises for any reason whatever.

Martina hurried to the bus stop and was just in time to get a standing position in a bus that would take her halfway to her destination. She asked a student from another school to hold her things and stood beside her holding on to the metal frame of the seat. She had overslept because she had been working on a project for Geography class which was due that same day. She hated to be late and knew that if it was not raining she would have to stand outside the gate and wait until the teacher on duty came and opened it, and then her name would be documented. If she was late for five times in four weeks then she would be given detention. Martina had only been late about six times in her entire school life and she had been suspended once when she had fought with Stone Cold.

When Martina got off the bus, she realized that it was raining a little heavier. The sky had a black angry look and the clouds seemed as if they were going to fall to the earth. When she looked in the distance, the hills were shrouded in black and she could hardly make out the silhouette of the houses. There were many people at the bus stop but there were no buses. The robot taxis did a thriving job as people got tired of waiting and were uncomfortable waiting at the packed bus stop with the rain blowing in on them. Martina did not like to take the robot taxis because of the many stories circulating about them. Moreover, if an accident happened, the victims would not be compensated. Martina noticed that there were quite a number of students among them, some from Milverton, who took the taxis.

The rain was getting a little heavier so Martina put her project into her bag and decided to see if she could push herself into one of the taxis. She finally pushed herself into one and found herself squashed among four other students in the back seat. There was only one adult in the taxi, all the others were students. Most of the students were from nearby schools. Martina was the one going the farthest and the lady who was travelling with them was the first one to get out. The driver drove speedily and did not participate in the conversation that went on in the car. He had the radio on and was playing dancehall music. The students shared all the information they had about the deejay and discussed the lyrics of the song being played. Martina did not participate in the conversation. Apart from the fact that she did not speak readily to strangers, she was anxious about being so late and was thankful for the rain because she could always use it as an excuse for being late.

Soon everyone got off the taxi and Martina was left alone with the driver. She could not see his face. His hair was in cane rows and he was wearing a black cotton shirt with a large yellow and orange dragon at the back. When he bent forward in the seat the dragon seemed to be snarling at Martina. There was something about that shirt that made Martina uncomfortable. The man seemed to be driving for a long time and when Martina started viewing the scenery through the car window, she noticed that it was unfamiliar. She felt a tightness grabbing her insides and sought to loosen it by telling herself that taxi drivers knew many different routes to various destinations because they were on the road everyday and travelled to many places all over the city.

After reasoning thus, Martina told herself that even if he was travelling on a different route it was taking too long. Fright again tightened her stomach and she decided to speak. Her voice sounded small and shaky as she asked, "Driver where are we going?"

There was no evidence that the driver had heard her as he did not answer so she shouted in a startled voice, "Driver I am late for school. Where you taking me?"

Again there was no response and Martina's heart almost stopped beating. She realized that all the stories she had heard of girls being abducted by taxi-drivers were floating in the fore of her mind. She inwardly recounted all the rape and murders she had heard linked to taxi men. Hot, angry tears gushed down her face and she wondered what he was going to do to her. Was he going to rape her and bury her? She tried to block out the agony of rape and death but it was as real as the fact that the driver was not taking her to school but to some unknown place. It was clear that his intentions were not honourable because surely he would have spoken to her or offered some explanation for his detour.

Martina could imagine the grief her family would have to endure. She knew that Miss Turner, Leonie, Hairnet, Terence and her new friend, Andre, would be devastated. It was strange that she even remembered Andre at this time, but since he had introduced himself at the first Debating Club meeting he always sought her out, whether it was lunch time, after swimming or if he should happen to see her anywhere on the school compound. He even came to her classroom on more than one occasion. She had promised to talk to him if he kept away from her class and he agreed. He always said and wanted to do kind things but she managed to explain to him that she was not allowed to take tokens from boys no matter what prompted the giving. It was strange that she should think of him at a time like this.

He was a male and if by some divine intervention she walked out of this alive, she would never feel comfortable around another male especially if she had to deal with them alone. Thoughts of Stone Cold rushed to her mind and she wondered if she would really be glad at her demise. She had been acting strangely since grade ten and had been unusually quiet at times, quite out of her character.

Martina decided to push away the thoughts and think of a course of action. She did not want to die and decided that if she had to, she would put up a fight. She had no weapon and she knew that her puny fists would be no match for the solid bulk in front of her. As she thought of the man sitting in front of her, she realized that she was sitting at the back and could try to jump out. She thought what if she jumped out and was crushed by the car or vehicles behind them. She decided that she would take a chance instead of just sitting there crying and waiting to die. She held on tightly to her bag with one hand and grabbed the door handle with the other. The man must have been watching her or had anticipated the action because he veered suddenly to the soft shoulder, stopped the car and then reached around and grabbed Martina.

Martina found herself looking into red bleary eyes and a large mouth with upturned lips which seemed to be trying desperately to contact the nose. The man had a dull brown complexion and must have suffered from a nasty bout of chicken pox in his earlier days because his face was dented with pock marks and some of the deeper ones had a few strands of hair growing out of them. His ears seemed to be in malice with the rest of his head, they stood askance as if they would take off as soon as the opportunity presented itself. Martina winced as large rough calloused hands gripped her shoulders mercilessly and yanked her forward.

The man spoke for the first time. "What you doing gal? Nobody and a mean nobody escape from Dragon!"

Martina had expected to hear a booming bass voice, instead a rasping squeaky sound was pitched at her. The man spoke as if he had a respiratory ailment which made talking an ugly, hurtful experience. He released her shoulders and then squeezed Martina's two slim hands into one of his. He bent over to pick up something in the front of the car and as he did so, Martina pitched forward, smothering her face on the car seat. The man, having found what he had been looking for, pushed back Martina on the back seat and tied her hands together with a piece of nylon rope.

The harsh realization that she was really in danger slapped her forcefully. The man was really in earnest about hurting her! When he spoke he was so savage and sinister! Martina went into a state of fright. She did not want to die. She wanted to do well at school and become something worthwhile. She wanted to become better at swimming and rise to great heights. She wanted to be around to help Yvette to be herself again.

She wanted to reach Shimron somehow and get him to stop taking drugs. Even though she was no expert, she figured that the vacant empty looks in his eyes was because of drug abuse. She had not figured out how to help him yet and even though she was not a Christian, she was praying that one day her family would somehow turn out right. Her mother was always not feeling well and she knew she would probably die if she was killed. Martina told herself that she had to find a way out.

Sometimes the will to live was much stronger than physical strength. Martina knew that she was no physical match for the dragon man, but if she used her head, maybe she would be able to save her life. Maybe she could come up with an idea from something she had read in a book.

The man drove for some time and Martina had no idea where she was. She was quite certain that they had left the city long ago as the buildings had become fewer and the vegetation had become quite pronounced. The road surface was not so good anymore and there were numerous potholes of ditch proportions in some parts of the road. Soon the man turned off the main road and drove onto a road which was more like a bridle path than a road. The sides were covered by quite a bit of dirt and only the narrow middle spoke of it once being asphalted.

The man quietened the engine of the car, came out and locked his door and then opened one of the back doors of the car so forcefully that the door squeaked in fright. He grabbed the rope and pulled Martina forward like an angry farmer yanking the rope of a stubborn animal. Martina jerked forward and almost hit her head on the glass. He pulled a curved knife with a silvery glint along the edge out of his pocket. Martina opened her mouth to scream, but the sound found no avenue of escape and stayed stuck in her throat. Even as the man used the knife to cut the rope from her hand, the scream refused to free itself and cowered just like Martina did before the man. He pulled her out of the car and she fell side ways against the door, scraping her shin badly. She had no time to utter more than a groan as the man pulled her up, held her hands and pushed her a little in front of him. He spoke for the second time that day.

"You see this knife? A have it right in your side. If you make one move you will greet your maker before him ready to accept you!"

Martina wondered if it wouldn't be better to do something and let him kill her than to suffer the double agony of being raped and then killed. As she pondered this, her pace slowed and he pushed her forward. They walked until they were in an area where there were large trees. They were no longer travelling on level land but were kind of going downhill. It seemed to Martina that the area was not altogether deserted as she could discern a narrow track going down that was not covered by grass as it would have been if it had not been frequented. As if to substantiate her thoughts, Martina heard the distant bark of a dog. A slight hope coursed through her, but it was soon dampened as the man pushed her in the other direction away from the far off bark. He must have become a little bit wary because he stopped in a little area where there were many shrubs among the trees. He stood, listening it would appear, for any other sound which might suggest the presence of humans.

When they moved off again they were still going downhill. The man stuck to Martina like tightly fitted clothes and at times he held on to her hand. The knife was always in his hand, exposed so that she would not think of trying anything. The path was slippery and once or twice, they stumbled. This jerky movement jolted Martina's thoughts and an idea like a faint light struggling to pierce the darkness came to her. Well, she told herself, sooner or later he will kill me whether I try to break free or not so I am going to try. She stopped suddenly in front of the man and as he bumped into her, she stepped sideways and used her aching feet to kick him. He made a sound, and tried to clutch at her, but she had moved out of the way so he could not get a grip. Before he could steady himself, she kicked him again. He lost his balance altogether and went sliding down the path using his bottom as a skateboard.

Martina did not hesitate to see if he continued the descent or broke it. She scrambled as fast as she could up the track using the nearby shrubs to keep her from sliding backwards. She felt pain cutting across her foot and groaned loudly. The pain had grown from a throbbing ache to a searing continuous pain. She suspected that it was as a result of the serious scrape which she had received from the metal on the car door. She had no time to stop and look at it but she knew it was swollen. She continued climbing up the track, dragging her injured foot behind her, not daring to look back. Finally she got to the top of the track and felt as if she could not move one step more.

The pain had become excruciating so Martina leaned against a tree to rest. As soon as she realized what she was doing, she chided herself severely and told herself that she must move on. Before she moved on she peered down the track. There was no visible movement and Martina wondered what had become of the man. Her eyes started to search the shrubbery and she spotted what appeared to be a bundle close to the bottom of the track. She wondered if it was the man and if so, whether he was unconscious, or injured. If he was merely unconscious, he could regain consciousness at any time and come looking for her. She decided that she was not going to stay around to find out. She knew that she couldn't go very fast and he could easily overtake her if he really got going. Moreover, he was familiar with the surroundings and could find his way around easily.

She started walking as fast as she could, dragging her injured foot and holding on to shrubs for support. There were little footpaths going in several directions and Martina took one which she thought would lead her away from the man. As she hobbled along she saw evidence that people sometimes came that way; branches had been chopped from trees and she saw small logs arranged like a pyramid. When she came upon this, she hid in some thick shrubs, thinking that at any time someone would appear. She had no idea what she would do if anyone appeared, especially if it was a male. After hiding for five minutes, she emerged from the shrubs and started hobbling again. She had no idea where she was going or what to expect. She needed help but did not know who she could trust. She started praying that some females would come along and rescue her.

A loud screeching sound jerked her out of her reverie; she hobbled in alarm behind a tree and breathed a relieved sigh as a flight of miserable, quarrelling birds rushed by. She must have frightened them, she reasoned. Maybe she needed to be much quieter as she moved around. For a reason unknown she did not move from behind the tree immediately but waited until the disgruntled birds had disappeared. She heard a slight sound opposite to the direction that the birds had flown and thought maybe it was the dog that she had heard earlier. She almost fell forward when she saw the man enter the section which she had just passed before hiding behind the trees. She asked herself if he had been following her all along. If he had been then why hadn't he overtaken her? Although she was petrified, she kept as still as the tree trunk she was hiding behind.

The man seemed to be walking away from her at first and Martina was glad. She noticed that he was going slowly and like herself, was hobbling. She was glad about that because if he should try to chase her, he would not be able to move very fast. What caused her to stiffen with fright though was the deadly silvery glint of the knife in his hand. Even though he had fallen, he must have held on tightly to the knife or he had retrieved it after the fall.

After walking away from her for a little while, he stopped and started to walk straight in her direction. She was about to run off when she told herself it would be better to keep still. Maybe he was just operating on a hunch and had not really seen her. As he hobbled across, he seemed to be staring right at her. Still, she did not move. He passed about two trees from her and as soon as he was a few feet away, she went around the other side of the tree. In doing so, he must have suddenly spun around and started back in the direction he had come from. Martina knew he had seen her. She gave a cry and started hobbling away from him. He made a strange high-pitched sound as he started after her. He told her to stop or else he would throw the knife at her, which he was very good at doing, but Martina paid him no attention. She walked in a crisscrossed manner so that taking straight aim at her would be difficult.

As Martina hobbled along, she felt a sudden sharp searing pain from her belly to her chest. She stumbled and almost fell. She felt giddy and light headed but kept on going. She knew without having to search for the answer that it was dire hunger announcing itself. She had been blocking her mind from the warning signals all along, but the hunger had refused to be kept at bay and was in full rebellion.

Martina refused to give up. Every time she looked back, the man seemed to be gaining because the pain in her foot and stomach had slowed her down somewhat. Desperately, she searched around for some way to get the man off her tracks. If only she could find something large enough to hit him with. As she moved along, her eyes searched the ground. Finally, when the pain ceased, her eyes alighted on a good sized stone. She bent to pick it up and fell in the process. She could hear the man clattering in the bushes behind her. She got up as hastily as the pain would allow her and hobbled into a clump of bushes nearby. She waited until the man was passing and aimed the stone straight at him. She felt like David and Goliath. The stone did not hit him in the forehead as David's had, but close to the back of his head. He groaned as he fell to the ground. Martina did not stop to see how much damage had been done but hobbled away as fast as the excruciating pain gave her leave to do.

She had no idea how long she kept going and every time she looked back she heard no sounds or saw no movements. Things were becoming very blurred and the pain had become unbearable. She barely stumbled along as if she was trying to pick her way through darkness or was a blind person in unfamiliar territory. At one point she picked up a few sounds but the fog in her mind would not allow her to distinguish the sounds. She felt a sharp pain zig zagging through her head and then everything faded into blackness as she fell to the ground in a heap, like a discarded bundle at the mercy of the elements and stray animals.

☙❧☙❧

Miss Fuller pushed the gate and walked towards the house. There was no light coming from the window and she wondered why Martina and Yvette were sitting around in the dark. When she started up the steps, she was startled when she almost bumped into someone sitting on the step. Frightened, she cried out, "Tina? Yvette?"

It was Yvette who answered, "A me mummy, Tina don't come home from evening."

"What you mean don't come home from evening!" Miss Fuller shouted, concern in her voice. Martina had always reached home by five o'clock and now it was after eight.

"No mummy is me alone here, Tina don't come home at all," said Yvette with wonder in her voice as she got up off the step and followed her mother into the house.

Miss Fuller turned on the light and passed through her room into the children's room looking around as if she did not believe Yvette. There were no bags or books on the bed or anywhere. The sheet on the bed was undisturbed because Yvette had watched television in her mother's room and had then sat outside to wait for Martina. After looking around and not seeing Martina, Miss Fuller felt emptiness and a low feeling inside her stomach. A pain started in her head, a different pain from the one she was already feeling there and in most of her body. Alarming thoughts assaulted her brain and she went back into her room and sat on the edge of the bed with her face in her palms.

Martina had always been home by five on the evenings that she had been at home. She had never really had any trouble with Martina getting home on time from school. She had always taken note of this as she was worried that she would become interested in men and lose interest in her education. She felt weak and lay down on the bed as she contemplated the idea. Was it a boy at school or someone else that she had gone with? She felt angry and disappointed at the fact that Martina had not listened to her advice about the deceptiveness of men. She had great hope for the girl. She was so bright and was doing so well in swimming. She knew that if she continued to take her education seriously she would do well and fight her way out of this place where they were living. She might even get some help as a result of her involvement in swimming. If she had gone away with a man then her life would be finished, ruined, at an end. She wondered if God was paying her back for being such a bad woman. She asked herself what right she had to expect Martina to be good when she was not. She knew she was a bad example but for some reason she had thought that Martina would make her proud. She groaned loudly, both in physical and emotional agony. The girl was obviously defiant because she had told her more than once that people in the lane would laugh at her, and she would never be able to hold her head up again. She felt sorry for herself. Her two older children had failed her and she wanted to die right away.

She lay that way until she sensed a presence and looked up to find Yvette standing beside her. She reached up and hugged her. At least she was still with her. She prayed inwardly that she would be for a long time. It was already past ten o'clock and still Martina had not come home.

Yvette interrupted her thoughts. "Mummy, we must go to the police."

"Police and tell them what? A not going to look fool fool when she turn up tomorrow from where she gone," said Miss Fuller angrily.

"Mummy, Tina not gone anywhere, somet'ing happen to her," Yvette declared, in a sad knowing voice.

"How come you know that?" she asked, turning fully to look at Yvette and noticing for the first time that the girl was crying.

"Mummy, Tina always come in from school early and do her home work. Somet'ing happen to her. I feel it here!" She touched her belly and looked at her mother, pleading, begging to be believed.

Miss Fuller looked at Yvette. It was a long time since she had heard Yvette speak so much. From the time she had gone to the country she had been lost somewhere in herself and had refused to come out. Her exuberance for life had faded and she was but a blurred picture of herself. She had become much attached to Martina and followed her around whenever she was at home as if she was afraid to be by herself. Miss Fuller had noticed that Martina did not seem to mind. She never told her to go away and always tried to help her with home work and tried to get her to talk. Miss Fuller looked at her face closely and saw alarm and fright and wondered what was going through Yvette's mind.

"Mummy, somet'ing happen to Tina. She want us," Yvette repeated, holding her mother's hand so tightly that she had to release her grip and then hold back her hand loosely. "Let us ask Miss Turner to go with us," Yvette persisted.

Miss Fuller went into her room with Yvette still holding on to her hand. She took up her handbag which she had dumped on the table, opened the door, went outside, and then locked it behind her. She did not like disturbing Miss Turner at this time of night but she knew that in the morning when

Miss Turner heard what had happened she would be angry at not having been told. Miss Turner always behaved as if Martina was her daughter and had great dreams for her future. Miss Fuller called and knocked at the door for quite a while before she responded.

When she did, she asked, "A you Fuller? Is what happen, somebody dead?" She sounded sleepy and irritated.

"Miss Turner is Tina. You have to help me!"

"Tina? Tina? Hold on there, a coming." The sleepiness was gone and was replaced by surprise questioning.

Miss Fuller could hear her moving around and soon she opened the door and ushered them in. Without waiting for her to speak, Yvette blurted out, "Miss Turner, Tina no come home. She somewhere out there."

Miss Fuller looked at Yvette in surprise. The girl had not spoken two sentences to her in all the time she had come back from the country. Her voice sounded strained and sad.

"Sit down quick the two a you and tell me what happen to mi daughter."

They had nothing much to tell except that she had woke up late and rushed out for school and that ten o'clock was gone and she had not come home.

Miss Turner shouted, "An' you wait till now to call me! You should a gone to the police long time! You know sey Tina always come home early!"

"But Miss T, you know what the police will say when me turn up there. First of all dem will say she gone off with boyfriend or it too early to declare her lost."

"Well I know Tina an' I trus' her and she not gone nowhere with anybody. Somet'ing mus' happen to her!"

Yvette looked at her mother triumphantly and then she looked away, not wanting to meet her gaze. In the next five minutes they were outside walking hastily towards Bigger Dread's house. He operated a robot taxi and they chartered him to take them to the nearest police station. At first he was reluctant to go because his taxi was not properly licensed and he had had several run-ins with the police. Moreover, they did not want to tell him why they wanted to go to the police. When they realized that he would not go unless he knew what was happening, they told him in one sentence. As soon as he heard, he agreed to help out.

When they arrived at the police station and made their report, they were asked the very questions Miss Fuller feared. Miss Turner vehemently insisted that Martina was not that type of girl. She took over from Miss Fuller and told the police about Martina's grades since primary school, the class she was in and why she had been placed there. She finished the glowing report with her swimming achievement. She stared the police sergeant boldly in the eyes and asked him why a girl like that would want to go off.

Miss Fuller had a small moment of doubt about why Martina would want to go away. She thought of hardships the girl had faced financially and emotionally, and wondered if she had really found somebody whom she thought could make things better for her. As suddenly as the idea presented itself, she pushed it aside. She would not allow anyone or anything to distort her trust in the girl's good behaviour. Maybe she had had an accident and really needed their help. She knew of the many possible things which could have happened but did not want to think of them.

As Miss Turner looked at Miss Fuller, she realized that she was even sicker than she thought. Her eyes looked sunken, her face had an unhealthy pallid look and she noticed, not for the first time, that she had lost weight. She had worried about her before, because she felt she was not telling the truth about why she was feeling sick so often and had to visit the doctor so frequently.

The police told them to come back the next morning if Martina had still not turned up and take with them a recent photograph. By the next morning everyone in the lane knew that Martina had not come home. When they had gotten back from the police, Shimron had arrived home and it was Yvette who told him what had happened. He had just opened his mouth and stared at her as if she had spoken in an unfamiliar language. He did not go to bed but sat outside on the step all night as if he was waiting for Martina to come home.

By the time they got ready to go to the police station and then to Martina's school, many people had gathered in the yard. They all looked sad and were acting as if Martina had died. Miss Fuller and Yvette looked at their subdued faces and started to cry. A number of women came forward to hold and hug her, encouraging her not to think the worse because Martina was a smart girl and would soon turn up unhurt. Mrs. Taylor, who was considered to be a real Christian, silenced everyone and commanded them to close their eyes for prayer. No one disobeyed. Even Shimron, who was standing by the doorway looking on, closed his eyes. Mrs. Taylor prayed loud and long, mentioning every part of Martina's anatomy and asking God to cover them with his blood. Because of the seriousness of the situation, no one sought to stop her in any way and bore with her to the end.

At the police station, the foursome (Shimron without saying a word had accompanied them), retold the story to the police woman whom they were instructed to speak to. They presented the pictures along with Martina's reports from primary school to high school. The policewoman was clearly impressed. She commented on the intelligent look on Martina's face and shook her head sadly. After giving some more particulars to the police, they left the station for the school.

At the school, they had to wait for over half an hour because the principal was busy with a planning committee. He realized that something was wrong as a result of the sombre look on their faces but was definitely not prepared for the news he received. After expressing disbelief, he immediately turned on the public address system and summoned the vice principal and the upper school guidance counsellor. When they arrived, he introduced Martina's family and Miss Fuller to them, and proceeded to tell them what he had learnt.

They all expressed shock at the news. The form teacher sent for Leonie and questioned her at length about Martina's friends and associates. The police arrived and were shown into the office. One of them was the same police woman whom they had spoken to earlier at the station. They asked the principal to try and find out whether anyone had seen Martina at all the day before. The principal, not wanting to publicize the matter, wrote several notes which were sent around to the different classes. After waiting for about ten minutes, a number of upper school students arrived at the office. They told everyone gathered that they had seen Martina at the bus stop. One was even able to tell them that she had what seemed like a project in her hand.

Two persons remembered seeing her board a taxi but when questioned about the vehicle and the driver, all they could supply was that it was a white Toyota Corolla station wagon. When asked if she had gone into the taxi alone, the students replied that the taxi was full of students. Not being able to supply any other bit of information, the officers thanked them, wrote down their names and the principal sent them back to their classes.

The whole family except Shimron was crying. Miss Fuller fainted and the school nurse had to be rushed in. The swimming teacher and the form teacher cried openly and left the office right after the nurse came.

Miss Fuller regained consciousness and soon after they left the office supported by the police; everyone followed. When they got to the foyer, a large number of teachers were gathered there. They looked on in painful silence as the police came through with the mother, the rest of students standing on the outside. Some were quiet while some spoke excitedly. Among the silent ones stood a tall young man with a straight face. He looked on as Martina's mother and family passed, their grief implanted on their faces. As the tears hastened to his eyes, he turned and walked briskly to the bathroom.

Over the next four days, Martina's mother became worse. She barely spoke and ate and it was the neighbours' encouraging words and prayer that really kept her alive. Every night when Martina's picture was placed on the television along with her description and excellent grades, she turned her face to the wall and wept. The appeals for her safe return made by the principal and her form and swimming teachers were not heard by her. Shimron did not go to 'work', but walked around the yard with a crazed angry look on his face. Sometimes he left the house for an hour or two and then he came back looking calm and far away. Yvette hardly spoke or left her mother's side. The neighbours had to force her to eat. The people in the lane were really supportive. There always seemed to be a number of them around, just standing around or going inside the house to visit Miss Fuller. Her cellular phone kept ringing, but she never answered it. Miss Turner took all the messages of good will and relayed them to her. The same two police officers came to see them everyday but had no information to share with them except that they were following a lead.

Very early on the fifth day, before Miss Fuller had woke up from a brief, unsettled dream filled with dark shadows chasing a little girl who became bigger and taller as she was being chased, and turned around quite often to laugh at the shadows, there were anxious persistent knocks on the door. Miss Fuller jumped up feeling very confused and afraid. She nudged Yvette, who was sleeping beside her, several times before she woke up. It was Shimron who opened the door and saw the two police officers standing there. He stared at them and blinked his eyes and could not form the good morning in response to theirs. His erratic heart beat caused his chest to shake and he looked at the police officers stupidly. His mother and sister, who by this time were standing behind him, could not speak either. The officers standing there seemed to be aware that the family was expecting bad news and understood the silence and the fear.

The female officer whose name was Miss Peart spoke. "Miss Fuller we have some news for you but we are not certain yet whether it is good or bad."

She paused and looked at the faces held by fear all staring at her. She continued. "The May Pen police have called to say that a young girl was found in the bushes in East Rural Clarendon and because she is so ill they do not know who she really is, but they are inviting you to the May Pen hospital to see whether it is your daughter or not. Please get dressed and we will take you there."

Yvette ran to call Miss Turner and in the next fifteen minutes, they were all seated in the police car and were moving out of the lane. Before they got into the car they had hurriedly told two of the neighbours, who in turn, quickly spread the news. As they drove away, Miss Fuller watched them conversing with other people who had run out of their houses at the appearance of the police officers.

CB80CB80

Martina's mother stood at the foot of the hospital bed watching her daughter. She seemed to be sleeping as she always had, everytime she had visited her over the past week. She seemed to be hardly breathing and looked so frail that if a zephyr should come along she would be blown away.

She remembered being teased about her thinness when she was a little younger than Martina. A group of amused, mischievous relatives had taunted her with the words "Straw eye, jump through needle, hide backa thread, and one little ants come pull her out." She had been so humiliated and wanted to sink into the earth.

As she looked at her daughter's slight frame, she wondered if she would live, and if she did, whether she would ever be the same. The doctor said she was suffering from a serious bout of pneumonia brought on by getting wet in the rain and lying for hours in the wet clothes. He also said she was anaemic and would have to be on iron indefinitely. There was a long deep scrape on one of her feet which the doctor surmised was made by her falling on something hard and sharp. It had become infected by the time she had been found and even though she seemed barley conscious at times, she kept kicking the foot as if she was in great pain. Overjoyed at her being alive, everyone was ecstatic when the doctor announced that she had not been raped. This had been the deepest fear of everyone and prayers of thanks had gone up when everyone had been given the news.

Nobody knew exactly how she had gotten to that lonely area in Clarendon. They surmised she must have been taken there by the taxi man but there was a big mystery surrounding the whereabouts of the man. The fact that she had not been raped and had been left alive was an even greater mystery.

Martina had not spoken since she had been found by two farmers and their dog. The farmers told the police they had been going to their coal 'skill' when their dog had ran ahead and started barking in a frenzied manner. He stood at one spot and barked and then jumped around barking in a circle. When they ran to the spot, thinking it was another dog or animal, they had been extremely shocked to find Martina curled up in a bundle. At first they thought that she was dead but one of them had detected that her chest was still rising and falling. She was thoroughly wet and they had wrung some of the water out of her clothes and had lifted and carried her for over two miles to their home. When they got there a crowd gathered and the women took over, changing her out of the wet clothes and rubbing her with alcohol and bay rum, and holding smelling salts to her nose. She had not responded and in alarm, one of the men who had gathered placed her into his car and accompanied by three women, first took her to the police station. The police had broken every rule in the book that governed safe driving to get her to the hospital before she died.

Her mother, after identifying her, had asked that she be transferred to the hospital in the city so that she could get to her much easier. That night the television news had reported that she had not been raped but was gravely ill. They had interviewed her mother, neighbours and members of her school community who had all given God thanks and expressed sincere wishes for her survival.

As the mother watched her, she wished that her life would be spared. She had so much potential and determination to succeed. She felt deep remorse at her accusations of her running off with a man. Even though she had not heard her story, she was convinced that what had happened had not been her doing. She was ashamed that as a mother she did not have as much faith in her daughter as she should. She had used herself and the life she lived to judge her daughter. She did not think that Martina was a saint but knew she had judged her wrongly. She had always been proud of her academic achievements but sometimes her quietness bothered her. She always wondered what was going on inside her head apart from her lessons.

One thing she was certain about was that not having a father greatly affected her. She knew the child felt unwanted and pushed aside, but could do nothing about it. As she stood there she was fighting a mental battle which entailed trying to wipe out the ugly details of Martina's existence. Seeing her each day was a constant reminder, but she balked at unearthing the painful details. Martina was far better off not knowing them, she decided.

As she struggled with her thoughts, her own physical secret ailment announced itself with a sudden pain in her abdomen. She almost fell but managed to hold on to the edge of the bed and closed her eyes until the pain subsided. Then she reached quickly into her handbag and took out two large capsules. She popped them into her mouth and washed them down with the remains of a box drink she had been drinking earlier. She then sat on the chair in front of the bed and tried to prepare herself for the nauseating feeling which always accompanied the taking of the pills. She put her head on her thigh and wrestled with the bad feeling and soon she slipped off into sleep.

She awoke minutes later and through a haze, heard voices nearby. She struggled back to reality and realized that there was a group of students standing solemnly looking on at Martina. She raised her head and they smiled shyly at her. She smiled back and quietly greeted them. One girl in the group who identified herself as Leonie asked whether Martina had regained consciousness as yet. Miss Fuller nodded no. The girl then introduced the other three members of the school swimming team. After the introductions were through, Leonie walked over to Martina and held her hand just like she used to do when they were walking at school together. Miss Fuller told her that she had to be careful that she did not dislodge the intravenous needle and only then did she release Martina's hand.

Miss Fuller noticed that she was crying and told her not to cry as she was positive that Martina would soon get better. In telling her this she was trying to convince herself. She had found that if she said it often enough it was comforting and gave her hope. She knew that Martina was a fighter and hoped that from somewhere in her darkness, she would find the will to defy her illness and live. She needed her to live for Yvette's sake.

The group of students left after putting a large bouquet of flowers and a fruit basket on Martina's table. Miss Fuller wondered who would eat the fruits because Martina was not able to even open her mouth much more to eat. As she stood there musing, another group of students and teachers came in.

After exchanging greetings with Miss Fuller, they did what everybody else did, stand quietly and stare sadly as if Martina would realize that they were there and rouse herself to make them happy. Before they left, a group of people came from her community. The nurse on duty ushered the first group out to make way for them. It was almost getting dark, the last group had left and Miss Fuller was about to go when a tall, athletic young man walked in. The nurse directed him to Martina's bed and told him that he had five minutes. He was carrying flowers. He greeted Miss Fuller softly and stood looking foolishly at her. He then asked her where he could put the flowers and she took it from him wondering why he would bring flowers for Martina.

After handing over the flowers, he went and stood over Martina, peering directly down into her face. For a moment Miss Fuller thought that he was going to shake her awake, but he only touched her lightly on the hand as if trying to affirm that she was really alive. He looked at her in a strange manner as if he had never seen a person so ill before. Miss Fuller wondered who he was because he was not in uniform. She also tried to figure out in her mind where Martina had met him. He appeared to be cultured and gentle despite his size and Miss Fuller was tempted to ask him who he was. He left only when the nurse asked them both to leave.

As soon as they were gone, a gentleman came to the door of the ward looking around as if he was not sure whom he was searching for. He walked inside haltingly, and then he walked over to a nurse who was attending to a patient nearby. She pointed to the patient four beds upwards and the man walked forward, still uncertain. He was a tall distinguished man, dressed in an expensive grey shirt and pants with matching tie; a pair of black shoes and a black attaché case completed the profile.

The nurse could not help but stare at the man. Visiting hours were over but she did not feel like telling the important looking gentleman that. She watched as he stopped at the foot of Martina's bed and then edged his way slowly to where he could see her face clearly. As he looked at the girl, his attractive mahogany face with its small eyes and well tended manicured beard exhibited no emotion. He did not touch her as some had done, but stared interestingly at her as if he was trying to form an opinion about something. It was hard to imagine whether he was feeling remorse or was nonchalant about the situation. She watched him shift from one angle to another as if trying to get a better view of the girl. As she turned her attention to another patient, she wondered if he was a media personnel or someone who had come to spy on the girl and then report back to the person or persons involved in her abduction. She did not see when he left; neither did she see when he slipped a small brown envelope under the heart-shaped bouquet.

Fourteen

Six weeks passed before Martina regained her health somewhat. She became conscious after the first week, and after the third week, she was able to move around slowly as if her feet were made of heavy metal and she was practising to move them and walk. The nurses took good care of her and grew to like the quiet undemanding girl who never complained but spent most of her time reading novels and text books even though she was advised against doing this. She spoke intelligently and seemed to be very well read, and the nurses enjoyed engaging her in short conversations on various topics. She formed a special relationship with the young policewoman who was assigned to the case. She felt drawn towards her and found she could speak as freely to her just like she could to Miss Turner.

Miss Peart, the police woman, through their talks realized that there were many things which seemed to be bothering the girl that she did not want to discuss. She did not pry or dig into her life because she did not want to frighten away the brave girl who was having a struggle trusting strangers. Everyone, after hearing Martina's methods of getting rid of her captor, praised her for her quick thought and action. Martina did not see it as bravery but as the natural inclination to preserve one's life which is present in human beings. The newspaper and television carried her story and she was lauded for her courage. A large number of people visited her, among them were teachers and students she had never spoken to before, community members and even the Member of Parliament for her area who had always paid her school fee.

She left the hospital after four weeks and was welcomed home by the people of her community with a party. She was very surprised to see so many people and the makeshift tables with food. They were playing music but her mother had warned them when they suggested the welcome, that she was not fully recovered and could not cope with too much noise, so the music was kept low. She also told them that she would not be able to sit up too long and would have to lie down after a while. Martina sat as long as she could through the strange merrymaking. During the welcome, she could not help but notice how thin, tired and ill her mother looked. She knew that her ordeal had added to her pain and felt remorseful about having caused so much worry.

She stayed at home for another two weeks and during that time she noticed that her mother seemed to have more money to spend than usual. She bought what was considered good food for the family and for the first time in her life, Martina had three good meals to eat even though she could hardly manage as she did not have much of an appetite. Her mother or Miss Turner always sat by her and insisted that she ate the food. Martina and Yvette got two fashionable dressing shoes and a few pieces of clothing for church. Martina suspected that the money came from people who had visited her at the hospital. They had taken her so many bouquets and she had taken home some of them with her. Martina hoped that her mother would not spend carelessly, but would save some of the money for her personal doctor bills and other emergencies.

She overheard her mother telling Miss Turner that she had not paid even a dollar for hospital bills because when she asked the receptionist for the bill she was told that it had been settled the morning of Martina's discharge. When she asked who had settled her debt, the receptionist told her that the young man seemed to be a messenger from an office. Miss Fuller did not question her any further but thanked God for all the help she had been given. She wondered if it was the same messenger who had left the brown envelope under one of Martina's bouquet. She did not tell anyone about the ten thousand dollars but put it aside for the operation she intended to have as soon as Martina was better. She wondered how long she could wait. She dreaded telling her children about the operation. There was enough sickness in one family.

On her first day back at school, Martina was accompanied by her mother. She had been advised to stay home another two weeks but had refused. She was strongly warned against resuming her swimming activities until all trace of pneumonia was gone and her strength had returned fully. When she got off the bus at the school gate, she felt like getting back on and returning home. She was certain that she wanted to get on with her education but was uncertain about the students' reaction to her. She thought of them whispering about her, probably thinking she had called down the misfortune on herself. She knew a few were genuinely sorry and had even wanted to visit her at home but she had deterred them. If she could help it, no one at her school was ever going to see her poor lane dwelling and spread her circumstances around the school. She had had a hard job side tracking Leonie and her new basketball friend from trying to find her home.

Everything seemed different as Martina went through the gate. Leonie, Andre, Tian, Terrence and some other students were waiting for her inside the gate. They called out her name and rushed towards her, surrounding her and almost causing the somewhat weak Martina to fall. She thought that at least they were glad to see her and felt a little better about meeting the others. Soon there was a crowd around her. Some of the students were just curious to see what she looked like and those who knew her wanted to see if she looked the same. Martina bore the attention as best as she could and was glad when her form teacher came and escorted her to her classroom away from the crowd.

While she was walking along, somebody offered to carry her bag and in alarm she hastily said no and clutched the bag even closer to her. She could not allow anybody at all to carry her bag. She had even asked her brother to buy a very small padlock for her. He had not asked her why, and eager to please her, he had bought two instead. She had packed her bag the night before and in the morning, she had made certain to put the keys at two different places on her person. She did not lock the bag while she was on the bus, only when she got off at the school gate. She had to make certain that no one interfered with her bag.

When she got to the classroom, she was greeted by a caption written in flowery letters on the chalkboard, "Welcome back to school Martina". She was very surprised and felt tears springing to her eyes. She felt as if she had been really missed and wondered if the idea had been the teacher's or the class collectively. She could not imagine Stone Cold wanting to welcome her back. She had noticed before she had stopped attending, that she seemed to have been a bit subdued, not altogether quiet, but not extremely talkative and a braggart as before. Martina did not want to continue the feud with her but she was certainly not going to offer to be her friend. Most of the students from her class were in the classroom but she was not there.

She sat and placed her bag on the desk and then placed her elbows on it. Many of the students came to her desk to say hello and ask how she was. She smiled faintly and told them she was feeling much better. Leonie stood by her most of the time as if she was her personal security guard. She soon noticed that there were other students from other classes coming into her classroom. Some looked at her and went back outside while the others came and said hello. Martina was not used to so much attention and started to wish that things were back to normal so that she could be herself again. It was not that she did not appreciate their friendliness but she found that she got tired easily and at the moment, wanted only to rest her head on the desk. She decided against doing that because she would only draw the attention she did not want to herself even more.

Soon the bell for worship clanged and the students rushed off leaving Martina and Leonie in the classroom. Her teacher had told her she could wait until everyone had assembled before going to the quadrangle. She had also told her that she did not need to stay for the entire time if she did not feel up to it. She did not wait until all the students had assembled because her almost solitary entry would cause all eyes to be riveted on her. She stood at the back of her line so that she could slip out easily when she needed to. After standing through ten minutes of worship, she whispered to Leonie that she had to go. But just as she was about to move off, the vice principal who was conducting worship finished praying and announced immediately after that Martina was back and asked her to come forward. She really didn't want to but she felt she had no choice.

Accompanied by Leonie, she walked up to the platform amidst much cheering. Without knowing why, she started to cry. She was barely on the platform but she could go no further. She held on to Leonie and for the first time since her ordeal, wept from her heart. The students became extremely quiet, as quiet as a new day making its entry when all living things were asleep. Martina's swimming teacher rushed forward and carried her away still crying. Her form teacher and guidance counsellor took her to the office and spoke as soothingly to her as one would to a baby. They all told her that they were available if she wanted to talk at any time. After a while, she composed herself and told them she wanted to go to her class.

As she walked back, accompanied by her form teacher, she realized how caring and compassionate teachers could be when one really needed help. Many times she had felt that they were unreasonable and did not listen as they should, but throughout her experience, they had been kind and humane.

Everyone stared at her when she entered the classroom and apologized to the teacher for being late and took her seat. She took her bag from under the desk and unlocked it, took out her book and tried really hard to concentrate. She knew that she had missed many lessons and would have to catch up. She knew Leonie would assist her with notes and she had already offered to write some for her in her spare time.

She wondered if she would be able to push her traumatic experience behind her and focus on her work. She told herself that she had always managed to do well even when she was hungry and family problems abounded. The family problems were not really gone, they were still there, nothing had been solved and she had only added to them. She told herself that falling back would only add more problems to her mother's burden. She could not let her mother and Miss Turner down, she told herself. She had to push ahead, continue the race she had started, continue with her swimming as soon as she could and go back to the clubs as soon as she had caught up with her lessons somewhat. She told herself that crying too much would not help, getting on with her life would.

At the end of school, she went to speak to her teachers about the work she had missed out on. When she was finished she walked towards the gate to find Andre waiting for her. She wished he would go away sometimes and not give the students the wrong impression about their relationship. She was now more wary than ever about males but she somehow did not put Andre in that group. He was always well mannered, although mischievous.

She could not understand why he wanted to talk to someone in her class when there were so many girls who would have liked to be in his company. Sometimes, they would give her envious looks as they talked together. She told herself they had no need to because all they ever talked about were sports and general matters. Her mother had asked her who he was and she simply told her a friend from school. He walked with her to the bus stop and did not leave until a bus came and she went into it. He had told her earlier on that he would ask his father to take her home, but she refused instantly, telling him that the bus was safe as there were many people on it.

She sat in a corner seat, close to the middle of the bus and started reading a text book. Every time she looked up she realized that adults and students alike were staring at her and whispering. She could well imagine what they were whispering about and she felt really sad. She asked herself how long it would be before people stopped talking about her and allowed her to try and bury the past. The whispering soon became audible as part of a nearby conversation filtered over to her.

"Is some of these young girls who cause the man dem to go after dem. Dem love money too much! Instead of sticking to dem lesson an' try to hold up dem head dem give dem mother pain and heart ache!"

The more the woman spoke the louder her voice became. Martina felt as if she could jump through the bus window. She asked herself why the woman was using other girls' behaviour to judge her. Maybe she had not gotten her story right! Her only crime had been taking a robot taxi and she hadn't done so by herself. It had been filled with people. For a time in grade nine when hunger had stalked her every waking hour, she had been tempted to go out of the way to get money. She had played with the idea for quite a while, especially when her mother had told her she would have to stay away from school because she had no money. There were always young boys and big men in the lane calling to her and making offers and she had been really tempted to succumb to one of them. It was the prudent words of her mother, Miss Turner and the guidance counsellor which had deterred her. How could she disappoint them, she had asked herself. After she had battled the temptation and won, she felt deeply ashamed and rebuked herself for even condoning the thought.

She was glad in a way that the woman had conveyed the contents of her whispered conversation in her ringing voice because it made her realize that everyone did not believe her story. Maybe some of the students who had stared at her at school had, but said nothing as they were also in agreement with the woman, especially those who knew she was poor. Even though Martina felt like retorting, she held her peace. She was glad when she reached her stop. She hurried out of the seat and walked pass the woman, fixing her with an ugly glare and wishing for the moment that she was Medusa the

Gorgon for she would certainly have reduced the woman to a sneering stone image.

After a few weeks, school resumed its regular rhythm. Martina worked harder than she had ever worked before at her lessons and swimming, and it was hard to tell that she had missed out on anything at all. She tried her best not to be absent even though at times she felt tired and only wanted to rest. In the Debating Club she was asked to be the third speaker of a team and even though she was nervous, she made quite an impression on the teacher and those who were present. She was having fun in writing too and was writing one and two verses of poetry. She was learning how to cope with the questioning glances and snide comments. She had discussed these with Miss Turner and she had told her not to be bothered because people would always question everything even when the facts are presented right in front of their eyes. She also told her that it was much easier to believe a lie than the truth. She quoted a thought which she had once seen written on the notice board when she used to go to school decades before, "A lie travels around the world while truth is putting on its boot". She told her that as she grew older it would make more sense to her.

CRWCRW

One day, close to the end of the last term, when Martina arrived at school, she saw a long line of students outside the school gate. She knew what the line meant and if the bus had not moved off, she would have gotten right back on it and gone straight back home. The children were being searched. They had their bags in their hands and Martina knew that they would also have to turn out their pockets. The male guards searched the boys and the female guard, assisted by three sixth form girls, searched the females.

Martina felt nervous and weak, her hands quivered as she clutched her bag tightly. She did not join the line but stood to one side and leaned on the wall. Some of the students thought she was ill and would have made her go in front of them if she had asked, but she did not. A frightened feeling rose in her stomach and made its way up to her throat, almost strangling her. She was breathing heavily, her palms had sprung water and she felt cold. Her only hope was a bus arriving at that time. No bus came; instead two teachers from the Physical Education Department came outside to see to the orderly running of things. All the students who were vociferous about being searched quietened down and straightened the line.

Martina fell into the line and kept her head down. The line became shorter and shorter as each student was searched and sent through the school gate. As she got closer and closer she became more agitated. No bus was in sight and even if one came she could not take it again, not with the teachers looking on. She felt like an insect caught on a sticky glue trap. She could not run but would have to take what was coming to her after she was discovered and delivered to the school authority. When her time came, she handed over her somewhat wet bag to the female guard. She averted her eyes while the search was being done and looked on foolishly when the guard gasped and called the attention of the three sixth formers to her find.

"My God! This girl? What an evil looking blade!" expressed the guard.

Everybody close by leaned forward to look and comment and then turned around to tell the other person behind. Martina felt like a convicted criminal marching off to do her prison sentence as she was escorted by one of the Physical Education teachers to the principal's office. She was told to sit among five others who had also been caught with knives in their bags or on their persons. They were all boys and Martina felt deeply embarrassed. They looked at her in surprise and one said in bewilderment, "A girl with a knife! This must be really a bad gal!"

Martina did not answer but took the seat farthest away from them and stared stiffly at the wall. She looked neither to the right nor left and ignored everyone and everything. It was as if they were mere whispers in the world to which her thoughts had taken her. Two more students joined them but she did not notice or care. She forbade the tears to show themselves, refusing to bare her heart in front of anyone. Some of those who saw her sitting there, staring thus with the determined, indifferent look on her face, thought she lacked remorse and commented on it. Many of them wondered why she had sought to get herself into trouble so soon after her ordeal, while some summed up the situation and knew why she had taken the knife to school.

When the principal came and saw her, he smiled at her, thinking she was there to see him about a private matter. He called her into his office and it was only after he had scanned the list given to him by the secretary that he realized why she had been waiting outside his office. He got up suddenly out of his seat and shouted, "You Martina, one of our best students, and a girl at that taking a knife to school! You had better have a good explanation or else you will be expelled!"

When he spoke he didn't seem so short anymore but reminded Martina of the man who had abducted her and the fiery threatening manner in which he had spoken to her. She recoiled, gave a whimpering sound and covered her face. The principal suddenly stood still and looked at the student in front of him. Something was happening here that needed more than a mere explanation. He told her to sit, picked up the phone, called the male vice principal and instructed him to deal with the other cases until he could find the time to help him. He then turned his attention to Martina. He wanted to call her form teacher but something told him that maybe the girl did not want an audience and would probably speak to him more openly if it was on a one to one basis. He lowered his voice several octaves, and in a soothing voice like a mother trying to coax her child out of danger, he spoke to her.

"Martina, kindly talk to me. Look at me and tell me why you feel that you should carry a knife to school."

Martina sat where she was as if no one had spoken. She still had her face covered and was as quiet as if she had fallen asleep. The principal did not speak to her again but watched her, deciding to allow her to compose herself and speak when she felt she could. While he was waiting, he started reading his agenda for the day. In his twelve years as principal, he could not remember one day ever going as planned, there was always something, however trivial, which always surfaced and pushed his schedule off. Some people thought that because he was the principal for a school which had some of the keenest students in the island, he did not have any problems or his problems were few in comparison to theirs.

It was true that some schools had more than their fair share of problems but that did not mean he didn't have quite a number himself. They seemed to have forgotten, he thought, that human beings were the same wherever you go. The good, the bad and the indifferent were everywhere except heaven and hell. In heaven there was only the good and in hell there were the indifferent and the bad. His school was not in heaven or hell so all three kinds were to be found there. In addition, the students were drawn from all rungs of the social ladder and came with their individual problems. He shook his head as he remembered the shoplifting incident in which the bright upper class tenth grade girl had been involved. Now this girl whom he had to deal with was definitely from one of the inner city areas.

When he had gone through her file the time she had fought in grade nine, the address had indicated that. Despite the address, the girl had worked hard and was doing quite well, the records showed. It was only the fight and this knife incident which had sullied her records. He had seen her in the pool and felt that she had a future in swimming. There was something about Martina that he couldn't quite fathom; there was a hint of finesse, a kind of gentle breeding about her which suggested a good background. Whenever she stepped out of line she really seemed to be under pressure.

He heard her sniffing and looked around. She had removed her hands from her face and was looking at him as if he was the offender and not she.

"Are you ready to explain your actions to me now," the principal asked as if he was asking her what time of day it was.

"There's nothing to explain sir, at least nothing that you would understand," Martina answered, not looking at the principal.

"Just tell me and see what happens," coaxed the principal.

"If I tell you, you will not understand sir. Nobody has ever attempted to rape or hurt you," replied Martina looking down at her lap, refusing to meet the principal's eyes.

"Do you mean that somebody has tried to hurt you again?" the principal asked incredulously. "Look at me and tell me what has been happening!"

"Not again, sir," said Martina. "I am talking about what happened to me weeks ago that some people choose not to believe."

"Not believe?" the principal asked in astonishment. "There was never any reason to doubt that you were abducted and managed to escape."

"Some people believed that I asked for it!" said Martina, angrily looking at the principal as if he was one of them.

"Tell me what you are talking about," said the principal. "I am afraid I do not understand what you are saying."

Hardly looking at him, Martina told what she had overheard. The principal could hardly believe what he was hearing. He told her not to worry and told her the same things that Miss Turner had told her in other words.

After he had admonished her, he said, "You still have not told me why you are walking around with a wicked, sharp knife and where you got the knife from."

Martina hesitated before speaking as if she was trying to choose the appropriate words to explain her action. After a while she asked, "Sir, if you feel threatened would you try to defend yourself? Isn't it a perfectly normal human reaction?" She looked fully at him, daring him to deny that he would.

He didn't answer right away as if he too was searching for the right words to say to her.

Finally he said, "Yes I have felt threatened many times." He paused then went on, "as a matter of fact I have been threatened. I will not tell you the details, but yes, I have been. But I did not walk around with a knife because that would only put me into more trouble. You see Martina, carrying a weapon can be good and bad. Mostly it is bad. It is good because it might help you to save your life, but bad because it can land you into trouble. You see Martina," he said, really getting warmed up to the counselling which he did so often, "if someone bothers you and you do not have a knife or another weapon it is much easier if someone is going to call you a coward. But if someone interferes with you and you have a weapon, your only thought is to use it to silence the person. Now you and I know where that will lead. What if everyone was to walk around with a weapon? If we all did that then we might as well abolish all the criminal laws and live like savages taking our chances whenever we can. You are an intelligent girl and I know how you feel but carrying a knife around is not the answer. Where did you get the knife?"

Martina did not answer at once. She was reliving the moment she had made her decision. It was right after she had gotten back from the hospital and her neighbours had held the party for her. She had overheard one woman tell another that she never went out without her knife because it was her protector. She went on to say that if Martina had had a knife she could have given the evil wretch what he had been seeking. She further declared that nobody was going to have an easy time taking her down. Her words had motivated Martina and she decided that she was going to do the same without anyone's knowledge.

She had searched around in the kitchen for a suitable knife but had found none except the two small ones used for domestic purposes. She found only the machete. Later in the week, Shimron came home early one evening before going out again, and she saw when he took the knife from his waist and put it into a bag under his bed. She waited until he was bathing in the communal bathroom, took it and hid it. When he came back into the room, she pretended to be asleep. He ate and went away not knowing that the knife was missing. Next morning she watched him searching agitatedly and knew he must be looking for the knife. She pretended not to notice and he didn't ask anyone for it. When she was packing up her bag, she had slipped it in.

Martina did not look at the principal when at last she answered. "I got it from someone," she said, refusing to go into any details.

"Well, Martina, that someone does not love you. I hope you will tell him or her that for me."

Martina knew that her brother loved her and would never have given her a knife. He would probably understand her motive because he must have been carrying a knife for the same reason as she had, but he would be angry that she had taken his knife. Martina would never tell him. She did not answer the principal.

After thinking for a while he said, "Now what am I going to do with you? I understand your reason for carrying a knife but you have done something very wrong. You have broken a school rule which carries with it the penalty of suspension or even expulsion, depending on your record. I will not expel you because you are a good student and I think everyone will agree with me that you have been through enough. I am going to suspend you for three days and I will not put it on your file because of the circumstances."

Martina could hardly believe what she was hearing. She would only be sent home for three days and her record would not be soiled. She knew that the offence she had committed warranted harsher punishment. She felt like hugging the principal and had started to say thanks when he interrupted her and told her that her mother would have to come in the next day. She told him that her mother was sick and could not come but he told her that somebody would have to come and represent her. Martina did not want her mother to find out because it would cause her too much pain and Shimron might find out about his knife. She would have to confide in Miss Turner and somehow get her to represent her without her mother's knowledge. Then she would have to find somewhere to spend the three school days. Martina thought she was unlucky and prone to trouble. So many things were turning out wrong in her life, would it ever end!

The principal told Martina to go to the library because he did not want her on the road by herself at that time of day. She went and sat in the library. The librarian knew her quite well because she was a member of the library. She sat in a corner, took out a textbook and tried to read but could internalise nothing. The words came and went like a mirage and she spent most of her time just staring at nothing in particular. She paid no attention to those who entered and left the library. The librarian did not seem to find it odd that she had been sitting there for the whole day, not even going out to eat her lunch. As soon as the bell sounded the dismissal note she bolted for the gate, caught the first bus and headed home.

The next morning she appeared with Miss Turner as her guardian. Miss Turner lied partially when she told the principal that Martina's mother was ill and had asked her to represent her. Miss Fuller knew nothing of Martina's problem or that she had conspired with Miss Turner to represent her. The only part of what she said that was true was that Miss Fuller was sick. She hardly left the house at all and when out she would be back home in two hours, which was quite different from the many hours that she always spent away from the house.

For this meeting, the principal was not alone. The upper school guidance counsellor and her form teacher were in attendance. Martina's charge was outlaid and the school's position on the matter declared. The principal did not ask Martina to defend herself but announced to all gathered the reason for her taking the knife to school. Martina was glad that he did not disclose any of the private conversation they had had. He repeated most of what he had used to admonish her the day before and then asked the other two teachers to speak. They repeated what the principal had said in other words. Her form teacher chided her for her lack of thought and pointed out that she knew she could achieve and that she should not allow anyone or anything to cause her to lose her way. The meeting ended with the verdict of suspension for three days for Martina and a fortnightly visit to the guidance counsellor's office.

Martina left home all three days of her suspension and pretended that she was going to school. Only Miss Turner and herself knew that she spent the time in the city's largest library studying and doing her assignments.

Fifteen

Grade eleven started with an air of urgency. It was the year of the big examination, Caribbean Examination Council (CXC). Martina was nervous, she wondered whether she could manage all ten subjects. She wanted to pass them all with credits and distinction, not the mediocre three. Her English teacher had told them that she was not expecting any threes in her class because nobody was majoring in forestry. Martina figured that this applied to all subjects. She was accustomed to working hard and earning good grades but she told herself that if she worked harder she would get even better grades. She knew her mother, Miss Turner and everyone else in the community were expecting her to do well and she did not want to disappoint them, especially her mother.

Her mother seemed to be feeling a little better sometimes. She had done an operation and was moving about again. Martina still did not know what was wrong with her. Her mother had only told her that something was not right with her belly. She had no idea what that something was but did not pry as it was obvious that she did not want to go into details.

Martina's new worry was her examination fee. It was due in a few weeks time and her mother became evasive everytime she mentioned it. She knew that the little money she had acquired during her abduction ordeal was gone into hospital bills. Her mother had told her not to worry because something would have to work out. Martina hoped it would because she would certainly end up in an insane asylum if after five years she did not get to do her exams. Life would not be worth living anymore. It would be better if she had died in the ordeal. Everyone would know of her rooted poverty when she could not pay for her exams. She hoped that embarrassing moment would not come.

Towards the end of the second week of school, Martina walked back towards her form room during the lunch break. Martina did not have lunch that day because she had decided to save whatever she could from her meagre lunch money to help pay for her examination fee. She was feeling a little hungry but she had made up her mind to bear it as much as she could. She was so busy delving in her private thoughts that she had no idea that she had almost arrived at her classroom door until she looked up. The place was very quiet and not unusually so because during lunch time no one was supposed to eat in the classroom because of the mess which the students normally made. Occasionally a few students who had opted not to have lunch would be in the classrooms but this did not happen frequently. As Martina got to the first classroom window she peeped in to see if anyone was there. She would be glad if it was empty because she could sleep off a little hunger before classes started again. She stopped abruptly when she realized that someone had gotten to the classroom before her. She could not tell why but she kept standing and staring through the window. The student inside was a girl. Her back was turned to Martina and she could not make out who she was. She seemed to be busy attending to something in front of her. Martina did not move but peered in closer trying to see who it was and what she was doing.

Suddenly it hit Martina that the student could be only one person. There were not many students with hair that colour which clung so closely to the head. Martina wondered what she was doing that engrossed her so deeply that she had not even heard her coming. The girl pushed something into her pocket and then moved on to another desk where she took up a bag. That desk was where Neil Avery sat. He often boasted that his father was a doctor and dressed to fit the role of the doctor's son with his expensive watch, shoes, bag and sports gear. He was friendly with the girl who was about to go into his bag. Before doing so, she turned around abruptly, uneasily. For a while she seemed to be staring straight into her eyes. Martina stayed where she was as stiff as a tree trunk, hoping she had not seen her. Seemingly satisfied that no one was around, she proceeded with her search of Neil's bag. She extracted some articles from it and then she moved on to another bag. Martina felt as if she was watching a film, not even if she lived to be as old as time could she ever conceive that this girl could ever be a thief.

She stepped silently back down the stairs before anyone could see her. She knew her propensity for getting into trouble. If anyone saw her when the alarm for whatever was stolen had been made, she would be implicated. She decided to go in search of Leonie and share her discovery but decided to first sit and try to make sense of the whole thing.

She had found out a few years before that her best thinking place was by the pool. The sight of the water always had a soothing stabilizing effect on her which lent itself to rational thinking. She sat on one of the chairs near the edge with a pensive look on her face. One mystery had been solved, she thought. She remembered when she had been maligned and labelled as a thief and the ensuing fight which had resulted. Even though she had no evidence to support it, this was the same person who had been stealing all along. She had been in the same class with her for the five years and had seemed so anxious that Martina be blamed for the thefts. What better way to divert attention from herself, Martina thought, than to get everyone else to think that someone else was the thief. Being thought of as a thief was something that followed you through life and destroyed your integrity, which to rebuild, was like constructing a building in water.

Martina had not once thought of that girl as a thief. She had so much and yet appeared to be a compulsive thief. What on earth was she going to do with all the items she had stolen? Maybe she would just throw them away or add them to her shrine of loot somewhere. Maybe she would just look at them at times and gloat about having outwitted everyone. What would her proud mother do when she found out that her beautiful, brilliant daughter was a thief? Martina wondered if she should expose her but no one would believe her without evidence. She decided that she would not tell anyone except Leonie unless there was a need to. The most bizarre thing was that she felt sorry for the girl! She didn't think that would ever be possible but she somehow was. She wondered if it had anything to do with the fact that the whole thing was so incredible and illogical.

She went in search of Leonie and told her the news. At first, even though they were such close friends, she did not believe her. Why, she asked, would someone like that student do something as dishonest as that? It was only when Martina insisted that she accept the information that she did. She pointed out to Martina that as soon as the items were discovered missing, the old story would start up again and Martina would probably be tagged as the thief. Leonie told her that the best thing to do would be to go to the form teacher and report what she had seen instead of confronting the girl and risking the possibility of starting another fight. Martina agreed with her even though she hated the role of being an informer, as anyone who told on someone was called. But when she thought about it she did not see why she should be blamed for dishonesty when she was innocent.

As soon as the bell rang for the resumption of classes, they went back to the classroom. The girls tried to behave as normal as possible, passing the student without saying a word as they usually did. They did not even glance at her, but went to their seats and started poring over their Geography notes as if they were studying for a real test. The Geography teacher came in and started the class. Her topic was "Weathering". She had gotten no further than the definition when Neil went up to the table and whispered something to her. No sooner had Neil sat down than Tavianne followed. Stone Cold picked up her bag and asked the teacher to excuse her from the class. Everyone sat, wondering what was happening.

As soon as Stone Cold got to the door, the form teacher, Mrs. Rowe, came up and sent her back to her seat. She refused to go, insisting that she had to use the bathroom urgently. Mrs. Rowe told her she was just coming from lunch and should have used the bathroom at that time. Stone Cold was almost in tears. The students looking on thought that the teacher was cruel and wondered how she would feel if the girl allowed nature to take its course in the classroom. Mrs. Rowe went over to the Geography teacher and whispered something to her. She shook her head and then went and stood at the back of the class while Mrs. Rowe took her place at the front. All eyes except one were nailed to her as she looked at the class with a serious, threatening look on her face and started to talk.

"There have been reports of thefts being carried out in 11m. May I see the hands of those people who have lost items." She paused and three hands went up. She acknowledged Neil and asked him to say what he had lost.

"A special ring given to me by my grandfather on my sixteenth birthday."

"Why you had to take it to school?" the boy sitting next to him asked, then hastily covered his mouth because he realized that he had spoken his thought aloud.

"That question is quite pertinent, but I will ask another. Who gave anyone permission to remove it from his bag?" said the teacher quite solemnly, daring the boy to provide an answer. Receiving none she went on. "You Tavianne, what was taken from you?"

"My partner draw of ten thousand dollars that I had just received before lunch!" Her eyes were filled with tears and it seemed as if she would start crying at anytime.

"Ten thousand dollars!" exclaimed the teacher, "why didn't you put it into your pocket?" She looked at the girl as if she was a qualified moron who deserved to have lost every cent.

"Miss, I had my phone in my pocket plus other things. Moreover, when I put things in my pocket I normally lose them. No one had ever stolen from my bag before. It is my money to pay for my CXC subjects!" She burst out into uncontrollable crying and two of her friends nearby rushed to hug and hold her.

The teacher shook her head in disbelief and then acknowledged the last person who had put up her hand. "Yes Camille, what have you given away?"

"Miss my trophy and my two medals which I got at devotion this morning are all gone." She looked with disbelief at the teacher as if asking her to confirm that this was impossible.

The teacher shook her head and said, "This person is obviously a kleptomaniac. He or she just has the urge to steal just about anything that can be stolen. I bet you the person has no real need for those items. Well, your teacher and I will be conducting a search right now. I do not know what it will yield but we are going to search everyone."

With those words the two teachers started searching. Martina noticed that Mrs. Rowe stood in the doorway as if she was anticipating somebody trying to bolt. She wondered why she didn't just call out the culprit and finish with it instead of everyone having to suffer the embarrassment of having to endure the intrusion of privacy. There were times when people had items in their bags or pockets that they did not want to reveal to anyone, not even their best friends. For example, Martina considered menstruation to be a girl's private business. She did not like exposing sanitary napkins. Two girls had to do that and the look on their faces had really shouted their embarrassment. They were also asked to take off their shoes and turn out all their pockets. A number of times the teachers had to make sudden retreats after being hit by putrid odours coming from some of the shoes. Even this did not make them give up the pretend search. Martina knew the teacher was just being diplomatic but the moment of revelation was drawing closer. The teacher's face gave nothing away, she searched each bag with the same expectant intensity, not speaking or smiling when odd items were revealed.

When it was Martina's time, she could feel eyes boring into her. She could imagine breaths being put on hold and tongues waiting anxiously to wag. Well, she thought, let them wait, pregnant with anticipation, hopeful, in suspense, on tenterhooks, eager to release their breath and accelerate their tongues. She revealed all the items in her bag, took out everything from underneath her desk, emptied her pockets and took off her shoes. No money, no ring, no trophy, no medals jumped out of hiding. Martina sat down and surveyed the faces peering at her. She could not really tell whether they were disappointed or not but at least two of them seemed surprised.

Soon the last row was left and Mrs. Rowe called out each student. Soon there were only two students left, Stone Cold and her friend Miscah. Stone Cold was called out first. She refused to move from where she was sitting. She was just staring in front of her with a bold disobedient look on her face. The children were shocked and wondered if she had not heard. They turned and questioned one another with their eyes and then turned to look back at the girl and the teacher. Mrs. Rowe repeated the order but Stone Cold's only indication that she had heard was to hug her bag tightly to her chest. She did not move, she did not respond, she only kept on staring in front of her as if something invisible and interesting was going on and only she could see it.

Mrs. Rowe strode in an enraged manner towards her, furious at being ignored in front of a whole class of students. Before she could get to the seat, Stone Cold jumped up, pushing the desk so roughly and suddenly that it turned over and almost hit the teacher on her toes. Mrs. Rowe jumped out of the way of danger and Stone Cold tried to use this opportunity to run through the door. As if she had anticipated the action, the teacher quickly spun around and grabbed at her. She held on to her blouse and there was a ripping sound as the material protested and gave way. This did not intimidate Mrs. Rowe as she grabbed the front of her tunic and tried to steady the girl. Still holding on to her bag, Stone Cold struggled with her. Her face now had a frightened, desperate look, like someone who wasn't really interested in struggling, but only wanted to get away. The Geography teacher came to Mrs. Rowe's assistance by coming forward and holding on to Stone Cold's hand. Like an injured, enraged animal, she wrenched her hand free. The motion caused the teacher to go backward, hitting her back on the chalkboard.

For a long while the students sat stupidly, their eyes transfixed to the drama taking place in front of them. Usually they would have whooped and beaten the desk in amazement or encouragement or purely for entertainment, but Stone Cold's behaviour had so astonished them that they forgot to do any of those things. Nobody moved, they sat as if they had become glued to their seats and as if somebody had robbed them of speech.

It was only after the teacher had been pushed to the chalkboard, that one boy got up and rushed through the door, slamming it behind him. His action caused the class to regain life and soon they were up, shouting at Stone Cold to behave herself. As the door was closed, Mrs. Rowe suddenly released her tunic and she stumbled backwards, losing her hold on the bag. It fell to the ground with a thud and before she could retrieve it, one of the students grabbed it up and handed it to Mrs. Rowe. Stone Cold lunged forward and started wrenching the bag from the teacher's hand. She was crying loudly and was so frenzied that the children feared she was going to hit the teacher. At that moment, the door was given a sharp pull from outside and the principal and female vice principal walked in. Their faces held deep surprise as they rushed towards the struggling pair. It took a great effort for them to control the girl. All three held her as she pulled and pushed and kicked out at the teachers in anger.

It took several minutes to quieten her and by this time there were many students crowding at the windows and doors to catch a glimpse of this rare entertainment. As soon as they had quietened her, Mrs. Rowe released her hold on her and took up the bag that had been placed on the table. Without looking at anyone, she unzipped the bag and tipped the contents on to the table. Everyone watching made a sound of surprise at the contents. Neil's ring rolled to the ground and a student took it up and handed it to Mrs. Rowe. Camille's trophy and medals sat on top of some books. The only thing missing was the money. The teacher turned out all the pockets in the bag, but did not find it.

"Now where's the girl's money?" she demanded of Stone Cold. The girl did not answer but started struggling with the principal and teachers trying to get free. After they had quietened her a little, Mrs. Rowe started searching her pockets.

"Get out of my pockets! Leave me alone! Leave me alone!" screamed Stone Cold in a pathetic manner which caused most of the children to laugh.

Martina knew that she should be laughing the hardest because she had suffered for almost five years because of this prejudiced, sick girl. But for some reason she could not laugh.

A strange feeling of pity came over her and she felt as if she wanted to take the girl away and hide her embarrassment. How had she fallen to that level? A rich girl who needed nothing materialistic had been stealing all along! There was no doubt in anyone's mind that the spate of stealing which had started a few years back could be attributed to Stone Cold. What was her problem? What had propelled her to malign others while she was the culprit? What had she done with all the items she had stolen? Did her parents know about her problem? When Martina stopped musing, she looked up and saw that Stone Cold had hidden the money in her pocket. She did not answer when the teacher asked her where she had gotten all that money.

Having found all the items, the teachers tried to get her down to the principal's office but no amount of talking and trying to push her could get her to move. The girl seemed to have garnered the strength of five people from somewhere. Even the principal's threat of calling the police did not shake her. She seemed to be at a point where nothing mattered anymore. Everyone stood wondering what was going to happen. The male vice principal arrived and sent the children to their respective classes. But those outside moved away only to double back in a few minutes and those inside the classroom insisted that their next class was inside the same room. The students had never seen anything like this before and they did not want to miss even one second of the action. The administration was at a loss, all they could do was to close the door and wait. There was not much talking and when there was, it was done in whispers.

After about twenty minutes, Stone Cold's parents came. They were shown to the classroom by a teacher. A number of children trailed them up the stairs, despite being told to get back to their classes. When the teacher announced herself and knocked on the door, Mrs. Rowe opened it. The couple entered the classroom and Martina stared at the woman who had given her the dirty look when she had had the fight with her daughter. Her hair was professionally cut and styled, and was offset by her costly peach and cream linen skirt suit which was also professionally tailored. Her cream leather shoes and handbag completed her ensemble. Despite the situation she had to face, Mrs. Stone, to Martina's surprise, did not seem greatly perturbed. There was no intimation of tears or any abashed look on her face. Instead, Martina saw a tired look of resignation which seemed to say "What can I do?"

Following closely behind her was a man who had no resemblance to the mother and daughter. Whilst they seemed to be white, he was what Jamaicans called a 'browning' (a Negro with fair complexion), but he was not the fairest 'browning' either. He was of medium height and was dressed in jeans and a short sleeve shirt. He had a straight nose with ruffles at the end and his face had bumps as if he was still suffering from acne. His eyes were sad. They looked deep and troubled as if he was about to cry. *Now he's the one crying,* Martina thought.

Without looking at the students, they acknowledged the principal, vice principals and teachers and went straight towards their daughter who was still being held by two teachers. The mother got to her first.

"What have you done now you disgraceful girl? Why can't you learn to behave yourself?" Her voice was trembling in anger and those present thought she was going to hit her.

"Why don't you behave yourself?" retorted the girl. Some of the students started to laugh but some people were so shocked that they could only look from one to the other.

The retort seemed to have incensed the mother more because she shouted into the girl's face, "Shut up, you disgrace or I'll hit you!"

"You are a worse disgrace than I am. Whatever I am I got it from you!" Stone Cold shouted back into her mother's face. "All you care about is yourself and your money! I hate you!"

At this point the father started pulling the mother away. She flung his hand away viciously and in the same motion, hit her daughter across the face. The booming sound echoed around the classroom and silenced everyone. Stone Cold retaliated by screaming and kicking her mother. She screamed as if she was being burnt or murdered. The piercing, wailing sound fled through all the openings and hovered over the school ground. Martina covered her ears and tears came to her eyes. She couldn't believe what was happening. It seemed like something bad that she had wished to happen to Stone Cold and not anything real at all.

She watched as several students rushed forward and held the screaming wild girl. The mother had fallen to the ground in a kneeling position. She seemed to be in pain but no one paid her much attention until Martina went forward, bent over her and timidly asked if she was alright. She looked up fiercely at Martina and the girl wondered if she remembered who she was. She seemed to be battling the tears and did not answer for a while. Martina offered to help her up and was surprised when she accepted the offer. She helped her to a chair and then focused on what was going on. The father was now pushing his way towards Stone Cold. He told everyone to give him some way and that they were to let her go. Nobody heeded him and he shouted as loudly as he could. "Leave her alone! Let her go!"

They all did. He held her hand and she did not resist. He spoke softly to her and she held down her head. She did not lunge or scream at him. He hugged her and she pulled a little away, looked at him and said, "Daddy I do not feel good."

"I know little girl. I know. Let's go home."

"I don't want mummy there. I don't," she started sobbing loudly.

"We'll talk about that later. Don't worry now."

He led her away, down the stairs and to their SUV without waiting for the mother, who was still sitting in the classroom staring at nothing in particular. She sat there for a long time and it was only after the principal spoke to her quietly that she got up and went downstairs with him. A few minutes later, she called a taxi and left.

Martina left school right after swimming lessons that afternoon. She was glad that there were several children at the bus stop so that she didn't have to stand out there by herself. Whenever there was no one at the bus stop she would stand beside the guard house until she heard the bus coming.

All the students at the bus stop were busy discussing the unmasking of Stone Cold. Already there were several stories circulating. One story was that she had been stealing since preparatory school and that her parents knew about it. It was said they had taken her to different psychiatrists but it only helped for a time, then she would start again. Another story was that she had been caught shoplifting a few months back and it was only because her father knew the store manager why she had not been arrested. They had kept her at home for a time while engaging another psychiatrist. Martina thought back and reasoned that that must have been the period when she was absent from school at the beginning of grade ten. Still another story was that her mother had had that problem when she was a teenager and that she was not as attentive a mother as she could have been. Martina did not join in the conversation and was glad when the bus came. When she was going into the bus she overheard one student's comment.

"You see that swimming girl that just gone into the bus; everybody did think it was she because of where she come from!"

Martina did not wait to hear anymore but made her way to the front of the bus and sat down. She was glad that the truth was out, that she had somehow been exonerated. She knew that some people thought that she was a thief but she did not know that the view had been so widespread. She still felt sorry for Stone Cold, even though the venomous girl had caused her so much pain. She must be really sick to have continued that way for so long a time if the rumours were right.

Martina was still trying to fathom the whole strange story when she got off the bus. She hesitated a little by the vendor's stall because there were talks that a group of boys from the lane had fired shots at some boys from the adjoining community as a result of a misunderstanding involving a gun. It was said that if the problem was not resolved then there would be war. Everyone was afraid. There had been peace between the communities for years. Martina was too young to remember the ongoing gun shots, the burning of houses and the lives that were lost before peace had been restored in the area. No one, especially the elderly people, wanted to ever see that happen again. Her mother had warned her to be careful and to be home early.

Martina saw no unusual activity as she walked along swiftly. When she got close to her home, she stopped suddenly. A blue pick-up was parked in front of her gate. Her first thought was that her mother had a visitor, but then for some reason she thought of Yvette's father. He hardly came to visit her since her so-called ghost invasion. Most of the time he sent her allowance via a family member or a messenger. Yvette had been slowly recovering, she spoke a little more these days but she did not keep any friends except for two from her primary school. She only went out with family members or Miss Turner. On the whole, she remained a quiet, withdrawn child.

Martina did not hear her mother's voice as she went through the gate and walked towards the front door. She did not want to intrude and went to speak to Miss Turner until the visitor left. After she had greeted Miss Turner, she told her that Yvette had collected the key. Martina did not seem to understand at once and then she said slowly and stupidly, "You mean that mommy is not there and Yvette is there all by herself!"

"Yes girl, so what is strange about that?" asked Miss Turner as if Martina had lost control of her faculties.

"Strange! Yes it is strange because there is a van by the gate and I don't hear any sounds coming from the house!" said Martina, sprinting down Miss Turner's step and rushing over to her house.

As she half ran and half walked she wondered why she had heard no sounds coming from the house. Yvette hated her father intensely. Before her visit to the country she didn't like him and merely tolerated him, but since her visit to the country the few times he had come to the house she had stayed far away from him and did not even look at him. One time she had become almost hysterical and had not spoken to anyone until several days later. Martina was not sure whose van was parked at her gate. The most likely person was Yvette's father and if it wasn't him then who was inside with Yvette? Martina had to find out.

She ran up the steps and burst open the door without knocking. There was no one in the front room so Martina rushed into their room. She did not see anyone at first because the room was a bit dark. Soon she made out two persons in a corner of the room close to the bed she shared with her sister.

Yvette was crying in the corner and she had an old vase in her hand. She had not moved when Martina had burst the door open. The person standing on the other side had. As she had suspected, it was Yvette's father. He was holding a piece of stick in his hand. Yvette was crying. Her face was twisted but there was a kind of brave determination on it. The vase she had in her hand was poised at a dangerous angle, ready to strike. The father seemed very surprised. He stared at Martina as if she was a stranger and had no right barging in on them.

Martina took a hard long look at the scene in front of her and a deep look of comprehension came over her face. She looked around for a missile and came up with a large old seashell that she had often used to keep her folder leaves from taking flight. She turned to face the father who was intent on edging his way out of the room. He stopped at Martina's word. "And what may I ask are you doing in here?"

"Visiting my child as I always come to do. Why you think you should question me?" he answered, trying to speak in an austere voice as one would to a rude interfering child who was behaving in a precocious manner.

Martina was not intimidated, if anything she became riled. "When mummy is not here you not supposed to come inside here. What were you trying to do with Yvette, your daughter?"

"She rude and I was going to punish her," he said, looking sideways at Yvette, waiting for her to contradict, daring her to speak.

"Rude how, by not letting you rape her again!" Martina said slowly, enunciating each word, allowing them to soak in and penetrate every fibre of Yvette's father's anatomy.

A shocked frightened look replaced the smug look on the man's face. It seemed as if he had been hit in the head by a huge rock or pierced with a sharp pointed object. Yvette gave a gasp and then started bawling loudly, uncontrollably.

"Wha, wha, what you mean? Who rape anybody? Gal wha, what you mean?"

"Mean! You soon fine out what I mean. You take the girl out here bout she must spend time with your mother just because you couldn't get to trouble her here. You destroy the girl, take away her life and you turn round and threaten her. Bout coolie duppy trouble her! You is the duppy, the rapist coolie duppy! You fool everybody except me!"

"Who you talking to little gal? Who you calling rapist?" He advanced on Martina with a sinister gleam in his eyes, furious at being exposed. Martina did not move. She held the shell ready to hit him if he struck her. Her sister had lost her exuberance, her love for fun and her childhood because of this man. She did not care anymore. She could not give her back what she had lost but would avenge her in whatever way she could. He rushed at her, hitting at her with the stick. Martina dodged and hit out at him with the shell. It connected because he emitted a low moan like an animal snarling. She hit him again, for the moment forgetting he was not the man who had abducted her.

A voice from outside caused her to raise her head. Yvette's father seized the opportunity to hit out at Martina. It caught her at the side of her left hand.

"Leave them you wretch! Leave them or else I will chop you up with my machete! You hear me? Chop you up!" Martina spun around. The voice belonged to Miss Turner. She had advanced into the room and was holding her well sharpened machete that Martina knew she kept under her bed for emergency. Even in the half light it gleamed wickedly.

In panic, the man moved away, dropping the stick and holding up his hand in terror. He began to sweat profusely as if he had been drenched with water. Martina noticed that there was blood on his hand and realized that Yvette must have hit him while she had been hitting him. He backed away from them but when he got close to Miss Turner he stopped, visibly trembling, not wanting to pass her at all. Miss Turner stood where she was deliberately, holding the machete menacingly, causing him to wet his pants. He kept holding up his hands as if he was warding off blows and then he sank to his knees slowly in a pathetic manner. Miss Turner looked at him and shook her head.

"Get out you dog before I use this on you!"

Yvette's father tried to stand, but fell several times before he was able to. One of the times when he went down, Yvette stepped forward and kicked him. He did not even look at her, but tried to get up. Yvette kicked him again and he used all the effort he could summon to get up. Miss Turner stepped out of the way and he ran outside, looking at her sideways as if he was expecting her to still chop him.

If the situation was not such a serious one, they would have laughed at the sad, sick picture of the fleeing offender. He almost hit down Miss Fuller who was coming through the gate. Miss Fuller rushed as fast as her slow limbs could carry her into the yard. She stopped suddenly when she saw Miss Turner with the machete in her hand. Martina and Yvette came out of the house just as Yvette's father pulled away in his van. They sat on the step and Martina hugged Yvette closely to her, she was still crying and she encouraged her to cry if it made her feel better.

Miss Fuller sat with them and demanded to be told what had been happening in her house in her absence.

Before the girls could speak, Miss Turner joined them on the step and said to Miss Fuller, "We been two big idiots. All along Tina was right. The only duppy that ever frightened Yvette was her father."

She proceeded to tell Miss Fuller what had transpired during her absence. She had followed Martina when she had sped off to see who was in the house with Yvette and had overheard everything.

Miss Fuller held her head in her hands and cried as if there was some force inside her pitching out water from a well. She was so overcome with sadness and embarrassed by her superstitious stupidity that she could not speak except to ask Yvette if her father had really raped her. The girl nodded her head but offered no details except to tell them that he had shown her a gun and threatened to shoot her if she ever told anyone. Miss Fuller told her that he would have to shoot her or get one of his friends to do it because she would not allow the matter to end there. Martina suggested that they speak to the police woman, Miss Peart, who had been so helpful during her ordeal and had invited her to contact her if ever she had a problem. Miss Fuller wanted to find out how Martina knew what had gone wrong with Yvette since Yvette had not told her. Martina told them she had used certain signs and her bookish knowledge that they had all spurned when she tried to tell them that Yvette's problem had nothing to do with any duppy.

The police woman, when she was confided in, said she had suspected all the time that something else was wrong with Yvette. She decided to question the father, even though she pointed out that too much time had passed and all the evidence, except Yvette's words, had been destroyed.

When she, along with another police woman, went to the father's home, his workplace and the places he frequented, they could not find him anywhere. His wife finally told them that he had left the country and she did not know exactly where he was gone or when he would be coming back.

Sixteen

Things were really bad for Miss Fuller. As she sat on her bed with her face in her palms, she wondered what she was going to do. She was feeling so sick that she could hardly even stand. After doing the operation she had felt a little better for a little time and then she had gotten worse than she was before. She could hardly even move around without feeling excruciating pain in the lower part of her body. She had also noticed that there was a little bleeding of late. She had felt alarmed and knew that there were two things she had to do.

She had started putting one together and felt compelled to finish it at that moment. She got up and opened a drawer and took up an envelope wrapped in plastic. She opened it and took out what she wanted and then she put the documents into a long envelope which already contained a letter. She licked the envelope and closed it and then she put back the other document into the plastic and put them away. She would deliver it that very night when she was going out. She had to go out for the last time even if she had to crawl. She just had to go! She hobbled to the kitchen and took her medication. It would help to ease the pain a little and then she would be able to walk better.

She went to her bed and sleep led her away into a hazy unclear world where some dead fish which had been thrown away came alive and started chasing the cat which was trying to eat them. They chased the cat up the tree and bit him. The cat screamed in pain and fell to the ground. The fish ran off and left the cat lying on the ground.

Miss Fuller woke up not certain what time of the day it was. She heard voices in the next room and realized that all her children were home. She looked at the clock on the dresser and realized that it was after six. Her head felt hazy as if she was not quite awake. She knew it was the effect of the medication she had taken. She would continue to feel a bit disoriented until it wore off. She had a little time before she needed to go out so she continued to lie down.

She was glad to hear her children talking together. She had given up on Shimron and was glad when he came home the two or three times per week. She did not know where he was the other times. She dared not ask him even though they sometimes exchanged a few words. It was after Martina's abduction that this had happened. It was strange how a crisis could bring people together. She wouldn't exactly say that they had been brought back together but at least he greeted her quite amicably whenever he came home. She often wondered why he hadn't moved out and guessed that he didn't have enough money to pay the living expenses. She surmised that some of what he made at whatever he did was spent on drugs. It was obvious by looking at him that he was taking some kind of drug. She had been around a while and knew how the drug users looked. She wished she could help him, but how could you help someone that you couldn't even talk to? How could you help someone when you needed help to get rid of your own bad habit? She felt that her life had been a hopeless failure and that she had not served her children well.

Yvette's voice came across to her. It was not the same Yvette that she had known as a small child but she felt happy to know that she was talking a little more, at least to Martina. Ever since she had spoken about the rape, she had changed a little, but not very much. Shimron had wanted to deal with her father himself but Martina dissuaded him. Moreover, as his wife had said, he had gone abroad and no one knew when he would return. The police had told his wife what he had done. She had been too shocked to respond in any way except to stare stupidly with her mouth open as if she was inviting 'whatsoever will' to go into her mouth. The police had extracted the promise from her that at the end of the month Yvette would get an increased allowance or else they would go public with the matter. She had hastily agreed. Miss Fuller knew that even if she hadn't, they wouldn't have publicized the matter because of the irreparable damage that it would do to Yvette. Yvette was telling them that she had heard that the boys, who were mixed up in the gun dispute, had decided that they were going to get serious about the matter. This meant that there was going to be trouble in the lane.

Martina was not saying much and Miss Fuller knew that the girl was worried about her CXC fee. The deadline would be the next week and the money did not seem to be forthcoming. Martina had told her that she had saved a little money from her lunch, but that could not even pay for one of the ten subjects. Miss Fuller had hoped that Shimron would have offered to help her but somehow he did not seem to have any money. His mother wondered what he did with the money he earned or whether he was really working at all. She would never ask him but would gladly accept it if he offered her some money. She had promised Martina that she would borrow the money over a week before but had not said anything to her since that time. She knew that she could not allow the most important part of the child's life to go by without trying to find the money. So many things depended on her passing her examinations. She would have to find a way somehow.

The medication was still affecting her and she dozed off again. She jumped up an hour and a half later and swore to herself that so much time had passed. She hurried to take a bath and as she went into the kitchen, Shimron passed her on his way out.

Twenty minutes later, she was ready. Martina and Yvette told her that her favourite show would be on in the next ten minutes. She knew they were telling her this so that she would stay home but she could not. She stopped at Miss Turner for a short while and then she went on. The pain came at her full strength as she was going through the gate. She bent, holding her stomach, and after a few minutes, fought her way to the bus stop. She was glad that a bus came right away and had empty seats. As it made its way into the thick of the town, she kept on glancing at her watch. She would only just make it in time with two minutes to spare. If she was late the boss would be furious and would want to punish her.

She got off the bus and made her way to a dark broken down building across the road. The only light that shone on it was the light from next door and the building in front of it. There seemed to be no one about. Miss Fuller walked as fast as the pain would allow to the back of the building. She seemed to know her way quite well because she did not stop to look around, neither did she bump into anything. She walked straight to the back where the putrid smell of cabbage and the piquant odour of ganja permeated the air. She gave one short tap, two long ones, one short and another long one and waited. Without a word the door opened and someone shone a flashlight into her face. Without a word she was handed a bag. She took the bag and left.

She did not go back to the bus stop but continued down the street. It was badly lit with a street light here and there. There were many potholes with water and mosquitoes diving in and out of them. Some of them sought richer food by perching on Miss Fuller's feet as she walked. But she walked on without slapping at them, thinking that the pain they were inflicting could hardly compare to the agonizing pain that tore through her abdomen and was threatening to bring her to ground level. Still she walked on, knowing she had only a little way to go. She must not fail now. Only a few people passed by, hurrying as if they wanted to get off the street. Only two vehicles passed by, their bright headlights illuminating the bad road and the decrepit condition of the buildings along it.

Breathing heavily, she reached her destination and stood in the shadow of an old building and looked around. She wished the person would come right away so that she could get to go home. A little cough nearby caused her to turn around. A voice whispered the word, "Sweetness" and she responded by saying "Honey". The owner of the voice stepped out of the shadows and she started handing the bag to the person. No sooner than the bag was out of her hands than a deafening blast disrupted the silence. Miss Fuller screamed and put her hand to her head. Another shot rang out and she bent to her knees and lay on the ground. She did not know how long she laid there. She could hear irregular breathing beside her but was afraid to open her eyes. She waited for a while and when she heard no other sound but the heavy breathing, she opened her eyes and peeped around, afraid that the shooting would start again and this time she would be shot for sure. Nothing happened and she fearfully stood up, looking around her wildly.

There was a small group of people standing on the sidewalk but they did not come forward. Miss Fuller started walking away. Then she looked back. The person was still lying motionless, his blue cap beside him. She knew she should try to help him but she was so weak, what could she do. She decided to go to the small group of people and ask them to help. She looked back at the person and in the dim light there seemed to be something familiar about him. He must be one of those that she often delivered the bag to. Just at that moment, a car came by. She jumped at the sound, remembering the two recent gunshots. The headlights brightened the scene and as she looked fully at the still figure, something caught her attention and she bent closer. As she shouted and screamed the name "Shim" she fainted and fell right on top of the body.

CRITICAL

A loud knocking on the door roused Martina from her fitful sleep. She had woken up twice before and discovered that her mother had not come home. It was after one and she hardly went out again, sometimes only once or twice for the month. Martina knew that she was very sick and had almost given up going out. She was bothered because even when she used to go out quite a bit she had hardly ever stayed out that late. Of late she was always home by about eleven. If she wasn't so ill, Martina would not have been so worried because she had grown quite accustomed to her mother not being around many times. Yvette was fast asleep on Shimron's bed because he too was not there. Shimron came and went as he liked so Martina was not worried about him. She had given up trying to find out where he slept and what he did when he did not come home.

She became frightened as she went towards the door. She knew that it was not her mother because she had her own key and did not have to knock. She had always been warned not to open the door to anyone. A number of times, some of the boys in the lane, knowing that Yvette and herself were alone, had pretended to be someone else and had tried to get them to open the door, but they were not answered. When her mother had heard about it, not from Yvette or herself, but the neighbours, she had gone cursing out in the lane. She had threatened to chop up anyone who came back to her house. That had been the end of that. She wondered if someone was trying to rouse her because of the conflict with the boys in the lane and the boys in the adjoining community. The knocking persisted and then a voice said, "Open up it's the police!"

The police! Martina panicked. Had something happened to her mother on the road? Since grade ten she had had her own notions why her mother went out so often. She had not really shared her opinion with anyone, not even Miss Turner as she was ashamed of the thoughts and more so the possibility that one day she would be proven right. She wondered if her mother had contracted AIDS but because of where the pain seemed to be concentrated, she withdrew the thought. She wished her mother would be straight forward and tell her the truth about her illness and her father.

She peeped through the window and saw two policemen. She felt ill immediately. An instant headache started and her hands trembled as she groped with the key. When she finally opened the door, she stood staring at the policemen, keeping them at a distance as if she was going to run. The policemen regarded her for awhile and then one of them spoke.

"Are you Martina?" he asked in a tone which seemed to be a little too polished for a policeman as they always seemed to be brusque and business like.

"Yes I am," said Martina in a voice that did not sound like hers.

"I am sorry to be the bearer of bad news, but I suppose somebody has to tell you." He stopped and regarded Martina before he went on. "Your mother and your brother are in the Public Hospital. Your brother has been shot and is considered serious. Your mother was found beside him. She has not been shot but seems to be seriously ill otherwise."

He paused and looked at the girl who had started away from him and even through her tears, he could see the mistrust and suspicion coming through. He stepped back, thinking that the girl seemed to be different from other girls of her age that he knew. She had an intelligent look and an educated voice. He continued, "Is your father around?"

"No we live alone with our mother. There is no man here." Her reply was straight, matter of fact.

"Well, you are going to need an adult to help you. Is there anyone?"

"Yes, my next door neighbour. I will go and get her."

By this time Yvette had woken up and was crying softly behind Martina. She held her hand in a comforting manner and tried to reassure her. She told her to stay while she called Miss Turner but Yvette followed her.

She roused Miss Turner and told her what had happened. Miss Turner kept crying and pacing the room. She kept repeating, "A know it would happen! A know it would happen!"

Martina tried to find out what she was talking about but she told her that it was not time to talk about such things. They went back to her house and collected items for her mother and brother and then went to the hospital with the policemen. On the way, Miss Turner tried to get details of what happened from the policemen. They did not know anything much except that people had reported hearing gun shots and when they went to investigate, they had found the two lying together in the street. They had no idea what they had been doing there and why Shimron had been shot. They had no idea that they were related until Miss Fuller had regained consciousness for a little while and had asked if her son was dead. She could hardly speak and the hospital official had had a difficult time getting her daughter's name and address from her.

When they arrived at the hospital, they went to see Miss Fuller first. She was unconscious and looked very frail and ill. Martina wondered how long she would last. She didn't even seem to be breathing. Martina hid her face in Miss Turner's back and wept. The doctor soon came and took Miss Turner away for a very private talk. Martina sat on a chair and held her head down until Miss Turner returned. Yvette was bolder and stood by the bedside staring at her mother the whole time.

When they went on the male ward to see Shimron, Martina felt as if she could not take anymore. Her whole life seemed to be at an end. She discovered that even though Shimron had been shot and was considered serious, he seemed to be in a better condition than his mother. Martina prayed that they would not die. If they did, what would happen to Yvette and herself?

Seventeen

There were only two days left for the CXC fee to be paid. Martina sat in her classroom wondering if this was how her high school life would end. As far as she knew everyone except herself had paid already. Her mother's illness had made her chances of entering for the examination even less. There was simply no money.

Both Shimron and her mother had been in the hospital for a week now and it was Miss Turner who had been taking care of the two girls financially and otherwise. She was as worried as Martina but had no money to help. Martina wondered if it was too late to go to the guidance counsellor for help. She also thought of asking the police woman who had encouraged her to come to her whenever she had any problem. She hated asking people for money but she could not just sit and allow her pride to destroy her future. Imagine attending high school for five years and leaving without any qualification. Her dream for sixth form and university would be all shattered. She decided to put them on hold because she knew she would have to try and find a job to take care of Yvette and herself. Even if her mother survived, she doubted whether she would be able to work again. How could she get a decent job if she had no passes in any of the CXC subjects?

It was the period before lunch and her class should have been having Literature but the teacher had not come to school. She was just about to go to the guidance counsellor when a student came with a message that they were all to remain in their classroom because the form teacher wanted to speak to them. Martina knew it had to do with the examinations so she did not want to face her teacher. She picked up her book and was about to go when the teacher entered the classroom. She sat down and waited for her name to be called. She would simply have to tell the teacher the truth.

When her name was called, she went to the teacher's table and stood waiting to be interrogated. The teacher started out by asking about her mother and brother. She then handed her the forms on which the subjects she had been recommended to do were written and asked her to double check for accuracy. She took the forms and noticed that there was a receipt attached to them. She looked from the receipt to the teacher in a quizzical manner.

The teacher noticed her look and then said, "Oh, you are supposed to get a receipt, this is yours to put away in case we lose the one attached to the forms."

Martina took the receipt and looked at it. The full fee for the ten subjects and the entrance fee had been paid! She was so shocked that she just kept looking at the receipt. The teacher noticed the strange look on her face and asked her what was wrong.

"Miss, who brought in the receipt?" Martina asked, wondering if some mistake had been made.

"I do not know the gentleman's name. He came in and asked to see me this morning. When I met him in the office he enquired whether your fee had been paid. I searched my records and told him no. He asked me what the sum was, collected the vouchers and returned them a little while ago," said the teacher, wondering why Martina had asked the question.

"Did he say who he was, Miss?" persisted Martina, eager to find out who her benefactor was.

"He did not tell me his name, but he said he was doing it on behalf of a relative who could not find the time to come himself. If you look at the voucher at the section marked 'Paid in by _____' you will see the name."

Martina did so but she had never seen or heard of Jervis Gentles. She did not want the teacher to see her consternation so she quickly checked off the subjects and handed the forms back to her. She went back to her seat feeling ecstatic. It was as if she had already passed her subjects. Who was this person and why had he helped her? Later that afternoon when she posed the same question to the happy Miss Turner, she could not answer it either.

Martina was doing very well in her swimming. The teacher told her right after practice the next day that there was going to be national tryouts and she would be taking her along with two others to this competition on Friday of that week. Martina could not believe she had heard right. She was so surprised that she almost hugged the teacher. She could not wait to get home and tell Miss Turner.

When she told Andre he simply said, "I know that was going to happen. I saw it long time."

She wished she could find a way to tell her mother when she went to visit her at the hospital that night. She ran down the lane both sad and happy, happy at her good news, sad because her mother could not share her joy. She rushed through the gate banging it behind her and ran towards Miss Turner's house. When she was almost there she stopped suddenly. Miss Turner was standing beside the steps holding Yvette. There was a small crowd of people standing by, looking very dejected. Some of them were crying. She turned around and started heading back through the gate knowing what she was going to hear but feeling unable to bear it. Two pairs of hands caught her before she got very far. She tried to fight them, crying as she did. They wrestled with her, and then held her close. One of them tried to soothe her by saying, "Hush, mi dear. It better she go to rest than stay here and suffer. No mind. God will help you." Martina screamed loudly as the woman held her closer.

CRUCRU

The funeral was over and Martina stood with Miss Turner, Yvette and some family members from the country that she was seeing for the first time. She had been very brave throughout the whole thing. After her initial outburst, she had decided that she was the oldest child (Shimron was still in the hospital) and should help to comfort Yvette and take charge of things generally. Everyone commented on the efficient manner in which she had helped to arrange the funeral and the way in which she had written and read the eulogy. Miss Turner knew that her mother would have been proud of her.

Both girls were now staying with Miss Turner. Martina hated to be a burden but was thankful that at least one friend was around. A number of relatives had offered to take the girls to the country with them but Martina had declined. She did not want Yvette and herself to be separated. In addition to that, these relatives were obviously poor and could hardly manage to care for themselves. Adding two more penurious persons to their household would definitely overburden them.

Leonie had told her that her mother said she could stay with her as long as she behaved herself, but Martina had declined. Andre too, had told her that his grandmother needed a young companion but Martina knew he was only trying to help and refused the offer. She was quite alright with Miss Turner. The only thing that they needed was money.

When the three got back home, Yvette went to sleep. Martina was glad because that would help the girl to take her mind off her problems for a while. Martina did not feel like sleeping, despite the fact that the past two weeks had been arduous for her. She went outside and sat on the top step, staring into emptiness. Miss Turner came out of the house and sat beside her for a while, saying nothing. Martina wondered if she was thinking about the extra burden she had taken on herself and how it was going to affect her life.

After sitting for a few minutes, she touched Martina and handed her an envelope. Martina took it and looked at her in a puzzled manner. Miss Turner saw the puzzled look, touched her comfortingly and said, "It belongs to you. A will leave you with it." She got up and went into the house, closing the door behind her.

Martina stared at the envelope in a quizzical manner. There was nothing written on the outside, neither at the back nor the front. It was properly sealed and showed no signs of anyone having tampered with it. It was not a new envelope and was a little creased. Martina kept on looking at it, feeling her heart making little jumps and starts as she did. Why had Miss Turner handed it to her and left as she had? Cautiously, carefully as if she was encroaching on somebody else's private affair, she broke the seal. She withdrew the contents and timidly opened it as if she was afraid of being reprimanded or as if she was expecting something to jump into her face. In a way, something did jump into her face; a passport size photograph, a birth certificate and a letter. Martina held up the photograph and stared at it. A young man about twenty odd years old stared back at her. He was wearing an afro and had small eyes, a straight nose and an intelligent, attractive look.

There was something familiar about him as if she had seen him somewhere before. Martina stared at him, wondering who he was. She turned over the photograph and saw the name Martin Patterson written on it. *Martin! Martina!* Martina said to herself. Why were those two names so close? She sat staring at the name and then she chided herself for not reading the letter and looking at the birth certificate. Certainly they would explain what the picture was all about. She smoothed the letter and started reading. The handwriting was familiar and right away she knew that it was her mother's. There was no date or address, it simply began with her pet name and continued in the same line. Martina felt as if her mother was speaking directly to her. She could picture her with her arms folded and her huge eyes looking at her, begging her to understand.

She read:

Tina. I know that I am not going to live for long cause of this sickness that I have and I have something a know you want to know. I did not live a good life. A set bad example and do things that a shouldn't do, but still for all, a love my children. A had 3 more an' they died when they born. Yvette was the last baby that live. A did not get along good with any of the father them so after a while a decide not to live with any of them. Some man is a worthless nation dem fool you up, promise you Downtown and Parade and when dem fine that you pregnant, dem gone, just like breeze or food that you eat and it stay in you stomach for a little time and then it ready for the toilet. Your father was a married man an' a was working at him house as a helper when him get me pregnant, but him wife suspect that something a go on an' tell me to leave. When a tell him bout you him threaten to shoot me if a ever call his name. Plus him say him would deny it even upon a Bible. Him run me and give me money to get rid a you but even though I am a evilous bad woman, I not a murderer. A keep you and I glad that a really do it cause you turn out so decent and bright like you father for him is a university man an' him have big post in one of the big company that deal with import and export. This is you right birth certificate and him live close to your school. You will need help when a dead so try and fine him. A love you like my life but God punish me because a bad. Hold up you head and let me feel proud in my grave. Don't forget Yvette and help Shim if you can.

Your eternal loving mother.

Martina stared at the letter as if her mother had finished speaking and she was not certain what to say to her in case she said the wrong thing. She knew there had to be an explanation, but she had not been expecting this. She was actually a whole human being with one of those persons called a father that other people had. Why had her mother waited so long to tell her? Maybe she really didn't want the man to kill her. Now that she was dead she suppose it was useless to try that. Maybe he would try to kill her if she confronted him.

Miss Turner came out of the house and sat beside her. Again she did not speak right away but waited for a few minutes. When she thought enough time had passed, she spoke softly, soothingly to Martina.

"A hope you got all the answer you want for a long time now. A hope you don't hate her."

"No," said Martina turning to her, "I don't hate her, but I need more answers. I hope you will tell me straight once and for all."

"A don't know everything but what a know a will try to tell you if it necessary," said Miss Turner with a wise look on her face.

"What was really wrong with my mother? What kill her? People whispering all kind of things," said Martina anxiously.

"She had cervical cancer," replied Miss Turner, not looking at Martina, not expanding, just making a statement.

"Oh," said Martina thinking, "I am glad it wasn't AIDS. These people 'round here think so."

"Well, that a their business. Dem ask me an' a tell them something already so..." Miss Turner replied, giving the impression that she was nonchalant about the people's view.

"Next thing," said Martina, "where does she always go and how comes she and Shim end up the same place?"

"A not one hundred percent sure, because she neva want to admit all of it but sometimes she deliver drugs an' sometimes she go out with men. Shim look like him was in the drugs business too."

"Something is clear now," said Martina shaking her head. "She never want us to wear shorts or go anywhere because she fraid we would be like her. She..."

"Exactly! Exactly! A don't blame her!" said Miss Turner vigorously.

Her questions finished, Martina sat quietly. After a while she handed Miss Turner the envelope. After reading the contents and exclaiming regularly throughout, she turned to Martina and said, "This one will have to work out. It have to work out."

CRBDCRBD

It did work out but in a much simpler way than the two expected. When Martina returned to school the following Monday, right after worship she was summoned by the principal. She wondered what she had done wrong this time. Her mother's death was so fresh and that wound would not be healed for now. She could not deal with any new problem now. She dragged herself rather than walked to the office. She took her time going up the stairs. The principal thought she looked very tired and depressed when he saw her at the top of the stairs. He tried to cheer her up by telling her that the school had decided to assist her by giving her lunch on a daily basis. He told her that they were aware that her mother had been the sole bread winner in the family. Martina was happy, even though she felt like a beggar. That meant that Miss Turner did not have to find lunch money for her. Thinking he was finished, she thanked him and started moving off. He stopped her and told her to go inside the office as a gentleman wanted to see her. She wondered if he had come from the Swimming Committee because she had missed the tryout because of her mother's death.

She walked into the office and looked around. There was a man sitting with his back to the door. She did not announce her arrival, but stood and waited. The man must have gotten tired of waiting because after a while he turned around impatiently. When he saw her, he stared at her as if she was an intruder. Then, recognition showed in his eyes and he stared even harder. Finally, he asked her to sit down. She did. She too had an idea who the man was. The eyes and the nose were the same ones in the picture. The face was definitely older, the afro was gone, but the features were the same.

Martina looked at him and boldly asked, "Are you here to threaten to shoot me as you did my mother?"

The man was shocked and visibly jumped. "So she told you about that. I wished she hadn't. It would have made things easier for us."

He looked a bit gloomy, but Martina was not sorry for him.

"Us? What us? Poor discarded mistake, me! How could I ever be mentioned alongside you. Don't you find that degrading, dehumanizing even?"

Her father did not grow angry as she wanted him to. Instead he looked at her in a strange manner and said calmly, "You are really your mother's daughter in terms of being spirited. But I have learnt that you are quiet, intelligent and very talented. You really do look and sound intelligent. When you spoke just now you sounded exactly like my sister. You not only sound like her, but you look like her and my daughter Sonjay whom you must have been told looks very much like you."

Martina felt the puzzle coming together. So that distant, indifferent girl was her sister and Tian was her cousin! My

God what a world! Those people who were always stopping to stare at her must be relations of hers. To think that this could be happening to her! She liked Tian, but her sister would definitely hate to be related to someone like her.

They stared at each other and then her father continued, "I have been following your swimming activites. You have inherited that talent from your uncle. He almost made the national team when he was at this school." He looked at her admiringly. "Your mother even gave you my first name."

"How did you know about me? I was supposed to be aborted, chopped up, become a medical routine! What do you want with me?" she asked unkindly.

"You really do have a way with words girl. Are you a reader?" he asked, ignoring her questions.

"Yes, I am. But what does that have to do with what I asked?" she persisted.

"Tian mentioned the resemblance soon after he saw you. I ignored him at first but one day when I saw you, and mistook you for my daughter, I knew you were my child. I checked back to the time when your mother had gotten pregnant and found your name and they checked out. I could not very well walk in and claim you because it would break up my marriage as it nearly did before. Now that your mother is dead, I have to help."

"But what if she had not died?" Martina broke in.

"I was planning to help you without revealing myself as I have done twice," he tried to explain.

"Twice, who did you help twice?" Martina fired back.

"I paid your CXC fee. I actually visited you in the hospital, but you were unconscious."

"Congratulations, you are a good father," Martina commented sarcastically.

He got up and looked at his watch.

"I have to rush to work now but I will be seeing you from time to time as I have made some arrangements between your guardian and myself. I know you do not like me but I hope that one day we will grow to like each other. One day you will get to meet your other sister and brother and other family members."

With that he left.

Martina did not follow him out but stood looking blankly in front of her. This was too much. She could not even decide within herself how she felt, but she had a father! She actually had a father!

Eighteen

Martina walked up to the podium and placed the folder with her speech in it. The graduating class was cheering and she felt a little nervous. She tried to get over this by adjusting the mike. Having done this, she started the preliminary lines, acknowledging those who were present according to protocol. Her voice sounded shaky for the first two lines, and realizing this, she delivered the graduation speech which she had written by herself, except with a few suggestions and corrections from her fifth form teacher.

Martina had been elected to deliver the graduation speech because she had done so well in her CXC examinations. She cried when she received the results. Miss Turner and Yvette had cried too. The people in the lane had been amazed at the slim girl with the big brain who had been through so much yet had succeeded. Her teachers were proud and encouraged her to continue. The person who seemed the proudest was her father. He had been robbed of words when he had come to Miss Turner's house to congratulate her. He had started providing for her and Martina was glad that Miss Turner did not have to bother herself to find so many things for Yvette and herself. He had arranged for them to live with an aunt of his in two of the rooms of her house. He had understood when she told him that she was not going anywhere without Miss Turner and her sister; Shimron had been out of the hospital for a while now and the kind police woman who had befriended her during her ordeal had enrolled him at a skill training centre and had arranged it so that he could live at the back of the premises. Martina had decided to continue her education in sixth form and had opted to major in the Arts. Very soon she would go to try out for the National Swimming Team.

When she was close to the end of her speech, almost everybody stood and started applauding. She could pick out the smiling faces of her brother and her cousins. Andre was also standing and cheering. Later, he would be her escort to the ball.

She ended with the words, "As you take your place in life, remember the struggles and the challenges you have gone through in order to be here this afternoon, don't forget that they are what make life worth living."